BASKET OF DEPLORABLES

Also by Tom Rachman

The Imperfectionists
The Rise and Fall of Great Powers

BASKET OF DEPLORABLES

Tom Rachman

riverrun

First published in Great Britain in 2017 by

riverrun

An imprint of

Quercus Editions Limited
Carmelite House
50 Victoria Embankment
London EC4Y 0DZ

An Hachette UK company

Copyright © 2017 Tom Rachman

The moral right of Tom Rachman to be
identified as the author of this work has been
asserted in accordance with the Copyright,
Designs and Patents Act, 1988.

All rights reserved. No part of this publication
may be reproduced or transmitted in any form
or by any means, electronic or mechanical,
including photocopy, recording, or any
information storage and retrieval system,
without permission in writing from the publisher.

A CIP catalogue record for this book is available
from the British Library.

Paperback ISBN 978 1 78648 874 9
Ebook ISBN 978 1 78648 873 2

This book is a work of fiction. Names, characters,
businesses, organizations, places and events are
either the product of the author's imagination
or used fictitiously. Any resemblance to
actual persons, living or dead, events or
locales is entirely coincidental.

10 9 8 7 6 5 4 3 2 1

Typeset by CC Book Production
Printed and bound in Great Britain by Clays Ltd, St Ives plc

For Matteo

Contents

I

Basket of Deplorables

Y OU CAN'T SEE ME right now. Then again, I can't
see you either.

One's hearing, they say, improves when you go blind.
Hasn't happened in my case. Not that I'm *longing* to listen
to anyone. But it's the election party tonight, everyone
gathering at our Manhattan apartment for the Hillary v.
Donald results. Actually, it's all going on now, right around
me, which explains my half-smile and nods, even if my
thoughts are elsewhere entirely.

Roger, my dearly beloved, has always wanted to be

remembered for famous parties. And his events *are* memorable, attended by literary types and pop-culture types – those he's signed to write books and those he's wooing. Christopher Hitchens was a regular presence, notoriously clashing with Henry Kissinger above a plate of quail eggs once. On another occasion, Andre Agassi and Brooke Shields turned up, squabbling like siblings, while the Saudi and Israeli ambassadors gabbed away like dear old chums. Even Britney Spears made an appearance, sitting on the kitchen counter and slurping from a huge bottle of Diet Coke, terrified by the hothouse intellectuals pinging her with questions.

But all such chatter halted roughly a year ago; tonight is our first party since my accident. Roger urged me to agree, said he needed this for work, for his reputation, and to mark the special day that America finally elects a female president. 'Could you try this evening?' he asked. 'You can still be charming when you want, Georgie.'

By contrast, my husband has no option *but* charming. He's a font of the right words, the right opinions, the right guest lists, the right seating plans. Only one feature is clangingly wrong nowadays: his wife, me.

When our guests arrived this evening, how uneasy they were after all these months. They expected my long hair, that luscious Georgina mane, uncut since age five. However, emergency-room medics had taken the liberty of shaving a patch at the back, in order to drill and relieve pressure on my brain. When recovering, I shaved the rest to match, and have kept it short ever since. Our female guests fibbed, saying I'm positively gorgeous with short hair – and their menfolk agreed with alacrity, evidently spooked by the sight of me so crumpled. When I myself had working vision, I categorized women just as mercilessly: a trophy wife, say, or a herbal-tea drinker, or yet another bipolar creative. Never did *I* belong in any category. But today? The gracelessly aging older woman who still smokes at parties? The kind who thinks she could still have an affair, that she'd have choices. Or did until recently.

I flinch at the warm breath on my ear. 'Bathroom break?' Roger asks, whispering that it's time for my pills, of which there are dozens daily. He leads me past our jabbering guests, neither my husband nor I speaking a word all the way to the bathroom, where I am freed.

I close the door after me, fumble for my pills, swallow them dry. I put my hands flat on the cold mirror, fingertips trembling. It's adrenalin. Because I'm *going* to do this tonight. In front of everyone. I will.

But wait. First, I must explain something.

It's immensely stupid, which is why I'm prevaricating. But you can't truly understand my predicament otherwise. It happened little more than a year ago. I was jogging up toward the Central Park reservoir, which I made a habit of lapping five times daily – not too shabby for a woman recently sixty. Just short of the park, I was flagged down by an anxious little old chap who sought directions to the Metropolitan Museum, which I supplied, annoyed to be interrupted while I had a sweat going. In his defense, there was nobody else around in the thunderstorm. So I outlined his route, whereupon he set off in precisely the wrong direction. Must be dementia, I supposed, and called to him, hopping backward as I did so, jabbing my finger north-east to indicate the correct path — upon which my brain shut down.

What followed, we later pieced together, is that I slipped on the wet pavement and crashed to the ground, the rear of my skull slamming into a steel gutter between two parked cars. There I lay under the pelting rain, unaided for forty minutes. By the time paramedics had me in their grips, the hemorrhage had wreaked irreversible damage: my brain went blind — not my eyes, which remain faultless, if pointless. It's the gray matter that can't see gray, or any other color.

Waking blind, I must tell you, is highly inconvenient. And it keeps happening. Because I see when dreaming. Then I open my eyes, and it's dark again.

What *you* likely fear about blindness is the loss of particular sights: trees swaying, or movies flickering, or your children's expressions as they age. But worse befalls you. You're suddenly surrounded by threats: each footstep the risk of another fall or crashing collision, as if thugs encircled you, baseball bats raised to crack your shins, knees, face.

There are lesser bothers, too. I dread the building elevator now. It's our neighbors there, each demanding a medical update. I will not hear myself yet again talking of 'damaged occipital lobes' and 'cerebral contusions'. I can't get better from this. *Stop* asking.

To avert such encounters, I favor the emergency stairwell, clutching its metal banister, sliding the back of each shoe down every riser to gauge the height, extending my leg, thigh and calf tensed – the terror of clattering forward twinned with a temptation to fall, as if on a mountainside, scurrying across a patch of ice, the void below. Finally, I reach our ground floor, where I invariably take one too many steps, finding myself in an absurd crouch, praying nobody comes to my aid, that the doorman holds his breath and stalks away.

Roger, I must say, has been impeccable. He bought me the talking microwave and the screen-reading software and a course on Braille, which I failed to attend. He gathered me up when I howled from our bedroom, unable to find the door out after two hours; he tolerates my mysterious headaches that last weeks; he ignores my hand-clenched rages. Yes, Roger is without fault – one of those men so handsome you assume they're stupid, though he most certainly is not. Only child of a Swiss banker and a French blue blood, my husband was born here in New York, raised in Singapore and Paris, attended Yale for good measure, and entered publishing thereafter, scraping by then at his dad's vacant penthouse. Strikingly fit for fifty-six, Roger retains a full head of salt-and-pepper hair and wears a frosting of white stubble, handmade suits cut in Florence, always a perfect white Hugo Boss shirt and a linen scarf around his neck, a different color each day. He speaks six languages with a proficiency ranging from native fluency to irritatingly excellent, knows food and wine and important people, and never overdoes any of them. What's most seductive is that Roger is *always* at ease. More than anyone I've known, he's convinced that he should be wherever he is. Including beside me.

So it was for sixteen years. Then I fell, and I woke, and it occurred to me: I have no connection to this man. When we were successful, that didn't matter. We were just the perfect match. I recall a scene from years back, when his daughter Scout, still a little girl then, walked into one of our parties in her pajamas, asking loudly, 'Daddy, who's smarter between you and Georgina?' Nervous titters ensued. However, there's no question anymore. Everyone just admires Roger – for his goodness in sticking with me, paying for the private nurses, tolerating the impairments. I'm a duty. An object here.

A burst of uproarious laughter in the living room. I reach for the bathroom light switch – it's been off this whole time; no difference to me. But I want the fan to blot out the noise of them. Gingerly, I touch the back of my head, as if bleeding again. My fingers trace the horizontal scar. How strange that 'me' is inside this skull. 'Me' used to be outside, wittily among them. Now I'm stuck in here, urging myself to do as I've planned. My mouth goes dry. Because I will wreck myself this evening. I will wreck us both.

Roger awaits me in the hall, and darts into the bathroom as I leave it, collecting my dark glasses, which I intentionally forgot. He hates it when I appear with exposed eyes, which fix sinisterly on people, dead blue monstrosities glowering at them.

He directs me to my place on the couch, where I'm engulfed by voices.

'What *I* don't get about chiropractors, osteopaths and physios is how they interface, you know?' Increasingly, our parties sound like a triage tent. The stage of life where people prattle about medical procedures, it seems, is also when they drift rightward politically. Coincidence? Mind you, everyone around here clings to the old leftie values, much as I wear jeans that are too tight, the only sign being that I tend to start arguments after a large meal. Thankfully for us, America has done us a grand favor in recent years, careening so ludicrously to the Right that we may drift from our Left lane and still consider ourselves radicals. Thank you, fly-over states!

'But what actually *is* the difference?' asks one of

our younger guests, the radio host and activist Vanessa Tejeda.

'If I may mansplain?' says the comic Andy Rosner. 'Physios have actual training, while chiros and osteos are essentially frauds with mystic beliefs in "alignment". They're found with some combination of scented candles, pictures of Mother Teresa, mandalas, dried-flower arrangements, and whale-noise tapes.'

Chuckles abound.

But, dear reader, I've failed you. I'm used to everyone but me seeing for themselves. However, you need narration, too. So look around: an apartment in Tribeca, open-plan living room, a half-dozen couches draped in Gujarati mir-ror-linens. Hardwood floors, covered by crimson rugs from Baluchistan. Twin industrial-chic coffee tables of upcycled airplane parts, the surfaces piled with fine-art photography collections and old copies of the *New Yorker*. Along the walls, floor-to-ceiling shelves, heaving with books. An antique map of the world. A few framed shots of my work, too – which is to say, snaps of pouty stars of yesteryear:

impish Liza chewing her green fingernails, Martha Gellhorn looking daggers, Truman Capote glazed after cocktails at Studio 54.

As for my work, I set out as just another posh girl in London, best known for drinking men under the table, taking my top off at parties, and being intimate friends with Mr. Jagger – a chain of facts that were highly correlated. I overcame this early infamy by way of New York, where I took magazine photographs of actors and singers and socialites. Which is how I met Roger, then a hotshot young publisher still at Taschen when he commissioned my first collection, *Vicious People Doing Stupid Things: The Worst of Georgina Peet, 1974–1991*. I can smell that first copy still, its gloss under my hand, each page sliding away as I turned to the next celebrity grimace.

Funny to think of those early pictures – already so acerbic, as if my Leica sensed what I was going to become before I did. But in the Seventies, a girl did need sharp elbows. Men were gropey then, and nobody much objected, except possibly the groped. Fortunately, I was skilled at bringing the impudent to heel. My mother taught us that anger is *the* worst tool. It's scorn you want, the colder the better. And I had a talent for it, honed by dismantling the egos of my older brothers, Hugh and Will, poor fellows. By comparison, pop musicians were a cinch. How they shriveled before my lenses!

My trademark image became the miffed star. I targeted my subject's security blanket and tore it away, whether it was a lurking manager, a circling lover or, later, a mobile phone. I'd drag out the shoot, playing on the celebrity's nerves, shifting lighting, fiddling endlessly with exposures, all the while prodding them, asking questions like: 'Are you still drinking as much? Or was that only after he left you?' Oh, how the pampered loathed me! But they had to contain themselves – a high-profile publication had commissioned me for the shoot. Only I could land them the cover.

'Think lava when you taste,' Roger is telling everyone, explaining tonight's booze: volcanic wines from Etna, Santorini, Tenerife – a choice esoteric enough to satisfy any *terroir* bores who might be present. The guests slurp appreciatively, nibbling mixed-seed lavosh with spicy feta dip, tossing back marinated olives and pimientos de Padrón. In the distance, the sound of Blitzer and his wolf pack emits from CNN, which is playing in the den, at the other end of the apartment.

A rule at our election events is that nobody watches live television – cable news is too excruciatingly IQ-melting. Also, if food spills on Roger's vintage Danish furniture in the den, he might weep. For the results tonight, we *were* depending on his now-overgrown daughter, Scout, who is monitoring the TV there. But in an antisocial slap against her father, she is refusing to walk the length of the apartment to deliver them, leaving us reliant on dispatches from her college love and companion, Emma.

Of our guests, I've already mentioned Andy, road comic of late-onset fame. He alone interacts normally with me tonight – flippant as ever, each of us ignoring the other but keenly aware. We've always been a little in love. Andy's a mess: scraggly beard, thick glasses, oversmart and not glad about it. I'm a decade his senior, but we might've been an item if we'd met back when Clinton the First was candidate and that name still represented 'youthful and sexy', as did I. Andy is two seasons into a Netflix single-cam sitcom, *Rosner*, in which he plays — hold your breath — a middle-aged schlub comedian. The show has made him what he calls 'niche huge'. Above all, it makes Andy a winner, which is deeply uncomfortable for him.

Reportedly, he came tonight wearing a T-shirt of Donald Trump with a circling American eagle, which was intended sarcastically, of course. That's the upside of Trump: he unites the sane. Sure, everyone has a deranged uncle in Kalamazoo or some such place blogging about how the Clintons molest baby pandas. But, hey, who didn't know that already? Anyone moderately coherent — including all those people you fell out with over the Iraq War — they're back on board now.

Our self-appointed therapist tonight is the aforementioned Vanessa, host of a hip WNYC show on politics. 'It's happening, folks!' she says, explaining Hillary's many routes to electoral-college victory. Vanessa has credibility, too, the only person here who has worked in politics, once a senior aide to Fernando Ferrer when he ran for mayor of New York City and lost to Bloomberg. Discreetly/indiscreetly, Vanessa is planning her house move to DC come January – Huma is a close friend. 'When the Republicans go down tonight, they'll hit hard on the voter-fraud baloney. Wait for it. It's the new Jim Crow. Seriously.'

Her approving chorus is led by David Ephraim, professor of cultural theory at Bard and one of Roger's long-time authors. His most recent volume argued that Americans ought to judge each other based on decency, not by capitalist metrics of success. This set off a shitstorm by mistake, when the blogosphere called elements of his book prejudiced, noting that David had cited a much-debunked study on race and intelligence. 'But not *approvingly*!' he insisted. The controversy was fantastic for sales, Roger told me, yet it nearly drove poor David to a breakdown since bigotry so contradicted his self-image. He kept apologizing on Facebook, but nothing stopped the blizzard of hate. Finally, it was Roger who saved the man, hiring an outside PR firm, and earning lifelong gratitude from his author. Seated next along is David's wife, Kiara Blonstein-Ephraim, producer of reality television, the socially responsible kind, most recently a series about trans teenagers in backward rural communities of the South, a show watched entirely by rich liberals in urban communities of the coasts.

To David and Kiara's left sits the Williamsburg fashion designer Sindy Pereira, who came tonight with her boyfriend, the novelist, playwright and *n+1* co-editor Enson Carthy. To readers, Enson remains the pretty boy of twenty-nine years old on the back of his 2002 debut, *Sugar Daddy*, a novel written from the perspective of a young bimbo trying to lasso a craggy old business magnate – a storyline that returned the book to bestseller lists this past year. Any similarity to Melania, he assures interviewers, is pure coincidence. Enson – closer to fifty now than to the waif in his still-unchanged author photo – hasn't written a novel since, too aflush with Brooklyn literary bling and magazine meetings.

Our biggest star tonight, as measured by Instagram

followers, is Sweet J Vincent, front man of The Late Jud Fry, an indie band of which he's the sole member. Roger just published a book of J's lyrics called *Poor Jud is Dead*, presented as poetry. He refers to J as 'the next great American singer-songwriter who'll be turning down an invitation from Stockholm'. A self-described OCD pescatarian, J is soft-spoken, tall and gaunt, with that fake shyness of the megafamous.

'Hey, you guys?' peeps a sniffly adolescent voice from the doorway – Emma in her role as second-hand CNN. 'So, Clinton just won Vermont.' Wiping her nose, she adds, 'But Trump got Indiana and Kentucky.'

Vanessa assures us that this is fine; as expected. 'Oh, you know Kentucky. It's red, through and through. We knew it was a write-off.'

Somebody touches my hand. A shiver passes through me.

'Just me,' Kiara says, squeezing my fingers as if I were Grandma. 'You're so quiet tonight, George.'

'I'm fine.' I swallow hard. Not like me to be a coward. I take my hand back, telling her: 'I was praying to Jesus for the right result.' This is irony, since nobody here believes in God, except possibly Vanessa, and she in a soggy, we're-all-one way.

Before Kiara can patronize me further, the caterers intervene, delivering appetizers to widespread *ooh*s: harissa lamb kofta bites with tahini and sumac; saffron rice with barberries, pistachios and mixed herbs; pan-fried mackerel yums with golden beetroot and orange hazelnut salsa. We always use this catering company, run by a Salvadoran whom we've grown close to. Lucio can reproduce from any cookbook – tonight, we have him raiding the pages of Ottolenghi.

J, our singer-songwriter-pescatarian, after loudly eschewing the lamb kofta, tells us that *he* actually knows America – he's toured the scary states. 'Don't you guys think it's possible something shitty happens?'

'Remember the Latino vote,' Vanessa answers. 'My people are winning it for you people. We get props tonight, you guys.'

'I'll just be relieved when this nightmare is over,' Kiara

says, informing us that whenever she and David go into conniptions over Trump they just check the numbers on the *New York Times* website, which brings them back to reality.

David demonstrates this on his iPhone, pacifying everyone with Hillary at eighty-five per cent probability of victory. 'They're saying: "Mrs. Clinton's chance of losing is about the same as an NFL kicker missing a thirty-seven-yard field goal."'

'What does *that* mean?' Andy asks. 'Does anyone have a clue how often an NFL kicker misses at thirty-seven yards? Least of all readers of the *Times*.'

Sindy, our much-tattooed fashionista, remarks that Hillary was at ninety-three before the Comey letter. 'Imagine if the FBI decides this election. Holy shit.'

Vanessa: 'Chill out! We got this!'

Enson directs everyone to the *Huffington Post*, which puts a Clinton win at ninety-eight per cent. Whoops sound around the room.

What Kiara would like to see is Trump absolutely

trounced. 'Like, publicly humiliated. Or does that make me a bad person?'

'Uhm, kinda?' Vanessa says approvingly, and the two women slap high-fives, giggling.

David's worry is that Trump won't accept his defeat, throwing the whole democratic process into chaos. 'I could see violence breaking out. Remember what he said about "Second Amendment people", how the gun nuts will have something to say about this?'

Sindy sighs. 'Can you believe someone running for president suggested that members of the public might want to *murder* the other candidate? Like, seriously?'

Roger is topping up everyone's wine. 'George, I'm filling your glass. I'm putting it in your hand. Close your hand. No, no – here. Right here. I'm holding it out for you. No, *here*. There we go. Well done.'

They pretend I still have a place in this party. In this apartment. In this city. We all know: I'd be in a nursing home were it not for my valorous husband. I don't have the funds to manage alone. I blew my money, as proof I could always land on my feet. Instead, I fell off them, and I cracked, worthless on the labor market, not to mention uncommonly frightenable these days. Is 'frightenable' a word? It's certainly a state of mind. Surrounded by this hubbub, I smell the nursing home, orderlies ignoring my room buzzer, the room-mate with Alzheimer's, a pitying visitor in our day room offering one-bite brownies: 'Take another. Help yourself. They're free.' You see, this is the bad side of never having had kids. Specifically, I'm told, you must have girls. They come home to nurse you; never the boys.

Of course, if I separated cordially from Roger, he'd leave like a gentleman, allowing me the apartment, paying for full-time assistance, too. I know him; he would. I cringe at the prospect – being nobody in a city that cares only for somebodies. I have one act of independence left, the last that anyone ever possesses: do harm. So, yes, Roger wants to be remembered for his famous parties? Tonight will be famous.

As I make this vow to myself, my palms immediately

go sweaty. I'm on the mountainside again, extending my leg over the void, marshaling the courage – just fucking go, George!

'Even *with* Hillary winning,' Enson says, 'it's horrifying that anyone in this country will have voted Trump. Our fellow Americans in Oklahoma or wherever, in the year 2016 – they wanted a *fascist* as president. Unreal.'

'Thank God there's no reason to ever visit a dump like Oklahoma,' Sindy reminds him.

'States like that shouldn't hardly exist,' Vanessa says. 'We should've let them secede back in 1861. Oops – did I say that out loud?' She snorts with amusement. 'But, like, Tennessee? And, like, Alabama? Do we really want those places in the Union?'

'Tennessee has a great music scene,' J notes.

To all of this, Roger offers agreeable purrs. 'What bewilders me,' he says, 'is that people aren't instantly disgusted by this man's narcissism.'

'Watch what you say,' Andy counters. 'Narcissism is America's second-favorite character trait after obesity.'

A few of the older guests bemoan the effect of social media, how it has normalized pathological egotism. Vanessa disagrees. 'Social media gives voice to submerged peoples. You get to say: "Hey, everybody, this is who I really am. I exist." Social media is taking ownership of the self. I actually did a show on this.'

'Definitely,' David says. 'Definitely an interesting narrative to unpack.'

If it's all the same to you, I'd rather just scream.

Meanwhile, Vanessa is in full fan-girl mode with Enson, saying how much she adored his novel *Sugar Daddy* when in college, and how she was also among the first to attend his off-Broadway musical *Purgatory!*

'I should give you a cash refund.'

'You weren't happy with how it came out?'

'Were you?'

Roger, ever the sunshine, observes that *Purgatory!* did get some positive reviews.

Enson corrects him. 'Everyone who matters hated it. But the producers wanted an ad in the *Times*, purely out of pride. So they tracked down some obscure online write-up calling it "achingly human!" or something. Like, what does that even mean? "Achingly human"?'

'I think that's from an Advil commercial,' Andy says. '"When *my* humanity is aching, I reach for …" Or was that Aleve?'

Kiara: 'If Trump wins, *my* humanity will be aching.'

'This rave of my play, it appeared on some nutcase website called "The American Standard" — one of those sites with ads for, like, gold bullion and survival bunkers and whatever. It's run by this hacker collective in Donetsk, basically to harvest money off Google AdSense. We're talking columns of blood libel about the Clintons plus random articles done by any loser willing to post without getting paid. Hence my "aching humanity" review.'

'Ah, the wonders of online!' Andy says. 'At what point can we all just admit the internet was a huge mistake?'

I blurt something, louder than I intended.

Roger touches my arm. 'George?'

I shake him off. 'I was agreeing. Isn't that what we're supposed to do?' Yes, yes, reader: I, too, shudder that the public might consider, from all eligible citizens, that ignoramus sociopathic billionaire. But I cannot stand how at these gatherings everyone must *agree* on everything. Gripping the thighs of my jeans, I take a breath, exhale very slowly. Damn well do this, George!

'Can't we elect Justin Trudeau for president?' Sindy asks. 'Have you guys seen that photo of him planking in the Oval Office, or whatever it's called up there in Toronto?'

'That guy is *hot*,' Vanessa says.

'Not Toronto,' David says. 'Montreal is the capital of Canada.'

I don't correct them, but I did once visit Ottawa, to meet the legendary Yousuf Karsh, when I was a young photographer and he a very old one. We talked shop, he boasting of that famous shot of Churchill, how he pulled the cigar from Winston's mouth before clicking. That gaze of bulldoggedness, it turns out, was merely a peeved aristocrat jonesing for his smoke. Before I met Karsh, I tried to make subjects look good. But, I learned, it's at their worst that you see people. So, can you see me yet?

'Even the Republican establishment is aghast,' David says.

Vanessa: 'After this, we're gonna see the G. O. P. redefine itself big-time. Mark my words. Tea Party craziness won't fly at a national level. It's the demographics, stupid. Republicans are out of the presidency for, like, forever at this point.'

Blindness isn't enough – I want to switch off sound, too, as my grandfather could, tinkering with his hearing aid during Christmas holidays at his pile in Somerset, we kids running wild, under the benign neglect of the English upper classes, where the worst peril was falling off a horse or perhaps getting blown up at the Somme. But nothing to moan about. When we children became too frightfully boring, Grandfather retreated to his silent haven. And I want mine now, so I close my eyes. Strange: I can't remember what my childhood looked like anymore. Not even my parents' faces. All I see are photos.

I open my eyes. Nothing changes.

Motion sickness overcomes me. I want to run, shouting, banging into coffee tables, fumbling for a window, punching through the glass with my bare hands. Instead, I remain planted on a designer couch. Dignity commands me to act; weakness gags me. So I bargain, making fatuous little wagers with myself. I'll obliterate my life here – but only if the words 'electoral college' are stated three times in the next minute. Yet when that tally is reached, I cheat, disavowing the bet, insisting it was too easy to count, and I formulate something else.

More bottles of volcanic wine are drunk; more full ones are installed. Additional small plates arrive, too: stuffed quince nuggets; eggplant boats with buttermilk sauce and pomegranate seeds; sea bream with beetroot, apple salad and dried Persian rose petals.

Our guests, excitedly awaiting the battleground states, distract themselves with petty polemics, such as whether circumcising boys is moral. David and Kiara are secular but had both of their sons snipped. 'It's a link to tradition for us,' she explains.

'Plus,' David adds, 'it *is* healthier.'

Andy: 'Oh, admit it, Dave, you just want your son's cock to look like yours.'

'You are a sick man, Rosner,' David says, through a chuckle. 'Where do you even come up with this stuff?'

Andy – himself absent from synagogue since his bar mitzvah – contends that David and Kiara lack any genuine link to the Judaism that their ancestors died to retain, and so they're paying for identity with their sons' foreskins. 'Here's what *I* wonder, though. The ideas of Christianity are pretty groovy, right? Be kind. Be forgiving.'

'As anyone can see from this great Christian country of ours,' J interjects.

'Okay, but the Christian religion does *sound* great, right? So why didn't all the Jews of ancient times buy into it? Here's my theory. This Jesus guy, if you met him, was an obvious charlatan, so only the suckers went for it. Who were the converts then? The *dumb* Jews – which got stupid out of the gene pool.'

Kiara, appalled, says: 'I cannot believe you're saying this.'

'Anyone with brains knew that dude was not holy. Be like, "Come on, Jesus! We grew up together, man! No way are *you* His son."'

Vanessa: 'Okay, so what's your point, Andy? Because you're kind of offending people right now.'

'I'm saying, maybe Jesus was the Trump of his day.'

'Did you just compare Jesus Christ to Donald Trump? Okay, now you got me mad.'

Roger intervenes, reminding everyone that Andy is a stand-up. He's professionally shameless.

'How wrong you are! I'm in a permanent state of shame. My secret is to keep shaming myself even more, so nobody can tell which bits I'm dying over.'

'All right then,' Sindy says, 'so what's *the* most shameful thing you've ever done?'

'On stage or off?'

'Anyplace.'

I murmur: 'I have something. To say.'

But nobody hears. They're already cackling at the lead-in to Andy's disgrace, which occurred at Johnny Carson's place in Malibu. Andy was just starting out back then, awed to be invited to the beach house after only his second appearance on *The Tonight Show*. He turns up, all aflutter, and Carson's maid tells him to wait on the divan, which is full of these fluffy cushions. Andy drops himself down, but it's super-uncomfortable, all pointy and hard under his ass. As Andy fidgets, Johnny sails in with a drink and cigarette, saying, 'Please, don't get up, my friend!' Andy – blissing out to be called 'my friend' by Johnny – forgets all discomfort. Carson is interested in me! He's laughing! After a half-hour, the maid returns, worried. It's time to walk Maxie, but she can't find him anywhere. Did he run out again? Johnny excuses himself, whistling around for the dog. Alone for a moment, the euphoric, red-faced Andy takes a deep breath and stands to fix his cushion – at which time he realizes he was sitting on a Pekingese, which is no more.

'You did not!' Vanessa shouts.

Carson's beloved pet is embedded in the divan in the exact shape of Andy's butt. In panic, he grabs the late Maxie, looks around – nowhere to hide him. Improvising, he shouts to Johnny that maybe the dog escaped on to the beach, and he'll race down there to check. Out of sight, the hyperventilating Andy flings the Pekingese corpse into the waves for a naval burial, wiping his hands on his chinos, dry-heaving from shock.

Everyone is convulsed with laughter, competing to ask Andy follow-ups. He bats these away, inquiring about *their* moments of shame.

I open my mouth again. But Kiara takes the floor, telling of when their sons caught her and David in bed doing a Dutch oven.

'Kiara! You are *not* telling that story!'

'Wait, what's a Dutch oven?' J asks.

'*Nobody* needs to hear this story, Kiara.'

33

'Is it something sexual?' Sindy says.

David: 'Absolutely not! Can we just drop this? We've got an election to watch.'

'Enson?' J says. 'Your face tells me you know what a Dutch oven is. Care to share?'

'Out of respect for a fellow author of Roger's, I cannot disclose.'

At which, the room falls quiet, except for soft tapping as everyone searches on their smartphones, followed by 'Is there no signal in this room?' then footsteps down the hall, then 'You did *not*, David!' and 'Ewwwwwwwwwwww!' and 'Why would you even *do* that?'

Tales of others' shame apparently relax our guests, for they settle cheerily back to munching Ottolenghi and gargling volcanics – apart from David and Kiara, who excuse themselves, supposedly to glance at CNN, though a hushed argument breaks out in the hallway: 'What in hell possessed you, Kiara?!'

Do something, I order myself. My pulse shivers; I remain still. To force myself to act, I concoct a fresh wager: that I will behave horrifically enough to make him despise me and throw me out of here – *if* the Americans prove so farcical as to actually choose that maniac for president. But I'm cheating again: the hyped-up Trump nonsense concludes tonight, after which the reptile slithers back into his hole. I've made a bet I can't lose. Or that I can only lose. I'll be sitting here all evening, overhearing everyone's triumphal hoots, me alone silent, a faintly embarrassing intrusion.

And I'm relieved. So relieved. My eyes well up. I get to stay.

The caterers clear plates, distribute fresh napkins, spread out the next course: five-spiced tofu with steamed eggplant and cardamom passata; gurnard baked in banana leaf with pineapple and chili sambal; baby carrots and shaved Parmesan with truffle vinaigrette.

'You guys ever think about the multiverse?' J asks, gulping down (and nearly choking on) a tofu chunk. 'Like, a version of this universe, but where there's no Trump.'

'Ah, yes, the multiverse,' Andy remarks. 'There are nice versions of me in the multiverse: an alternative

Andy Rosner, drinking caramel Frappuccinos and feeling people's pain.'

'Would the multiverse theory account for something that unlikely?' Vanessa quips. 'Even with an infinite number of universes, I'd find that a little hard to buy.'

'Hey, you guys?' It's Kiara, breathless, back from the den.

David is there, too, sounding like his Prius just flipped into a ditch. 'You guys, Trump won Ohio.'

Anxious throat-clearing ensues, everyone trying to recall what Ohio means, where it even is. Vanessa assures us that Trump did a ton of campaigning there. This isn't shocking.

'That's the first swing state, right?' J notes. 'And it went Republican.'

'Things looked sweet for Romney at one point,' Vanessa reminds us. 'It's just Ohio, guys. Hillary's got this.'

Lighting a cigarette, J steps on to the fire escape to tweet off some steam.

I feel around for my wine glass but can't find it. My feet are tapping under the coffee table, thinking of my wager.

A quarter-hour later, Emma squeaks at us from the doorway: 'Virginia's in. It went Clinton.'

Shrieks of relief.

'Do *not* screw this up, Hillary!' Enson says.

It's 270 electoral votes to win the presidency, and CNN now has Trump at 167 with Clinton at 122.

J, back among us, is still tense. 'I'm not loving the look of this.'

'Can you guys be positive?' Vanessa says. 'Please?'

Minutes later, Emma returns. 'Clinton takes Colorado.'

Sindy whoops. 'Keep 'em coming, baby!'

'See?' Vanessa says. 'We'll nail Michigan next. Ignore all the early-reporting counties. They always go Republican.'

After protracted chatter about network projections and absentee ballots and day-of turnout, Emma swoops back in: 'North Carolina's important, right?'

'Emma! Suspense is *not* funny right now, okay?'

'It's gone Trump.'

Gasps.

Enson unleashes a flurry of creative cursing, then rants

about Hillary being a terrible candidate, that we should *not* be facing a cliffhanger against a psycho like Trump. A call-and-response develops, someone casting blame – Russian hacking, or WikiLeaks, or misogyny, or racism, or the media – and Vanessa assuring everyone that we still got this.

Indeed, as the night drags on, Clinton's electoral votes add up nicely. She's above Trump now, 197 to 187, and well poised in Michigan. 'We're clawing back,' Vanessa says. 'First woman president. You heard it here, guys.'

Emma bursts in.

'Behold, ye angel of death,' Andy says. 'What news from the dark side?'

'So, Florida's a big deal, right?'

'What happened, Emma? Don't do this!'

'CNN has its projection.'

'Tell us!'

'Trump.'

Apocalyptic howls.

'No!'

'No!'

'No, no, no!'

'I am not hearing this!'

'Say you're messing with us right now.'

'Jesus H. Christ! Trump could do this!' Enson exclaims. 'He could actually take this.'

A peculiar calm overcomes me, and I'm almost as I used to be. Because I'm tired. Tired of waiting. Tired of myself. Burn it down, everything.

'This is *not* over yet,' Vanessa insists. We don't have final results yet from Pennsylvania. Or Wisconsin. And Michigan's still wide open.

'It's over,' I tell her.

'No, Georgina, everything's okay still,' Kiara says, as if to a five-year-old. 'A bunch of states still to come in. And he's not got enough electoral-college votes yet.'

'Your moronic electoral college. Can't you just have a fucking winner? I have to wait all night for this?'

An uncomfortable silence follows, the guests noticing their impaired hostess.

David breaks the tension by reaming out his iPhone because the *Times* app betrayed America. 'How can they say Hillary was romping home three hours ago? And now a Trump win is at seventy-two per cent? What the hell?'

David and Vanessa hurry away to eyeball CNN, dashing back every few minutes to relate the latest. Over a couple of fraught hours, Trump takes Georgia, Iowa, Utah. He's at 244 electoral votes, Clinton at 215.

The caterers spread out dessert, Lucio and his team superbly polite, as if this were any other evening. Somebody whispers to the other guests: 'You think the waiters are undocumented? How can Trump say illegals don't contribute anything?' In particular: ricotta fritters with blackberry sauce and chocolate soil; sweet filo cigars; popcorn ice cream with caramelized black pepper. But nobody praises the desserts. Just fast-chewing, fast-swallowing. Someone hammer-fists a coffee table. Others speculate that Bernie wudda had this; he wudda. Biden, easily. Don't even mention Elizabeth Warren.

Dutifully, David responds, 'We're not done yet.'

'Hillary was right,' Andy says. 'It *was* a basket of deplorables. Only a very, very large basket.'

Roger frees anyone to go stare at CNN, if they so desire.

'Why is nobody answering?' I ask.

From the hall, J calls back: 'We're all on our phones, playing "fuck" tennis.'

'What is "fuck" tennis?'

'Texting "fuck" to everyone you know, and them texting "fuck" back.'

'Where are you, Roger?' I say.

'Right here.'

Chest pattering, I wipe my mouth. And suddenly, I've begun – speaking too hurriedly, then too slowly, jaw tight and throat parched, as if delivering a speech to a packed, darkened auditorium. '... years back, on vacation with my boyfriend, down in the south of Italy, back when nobody went to those parts. All red earth and olive trees – very dry, very poor. We went to this beach, my then boyfriend and I, and then drove on to Lecce, ate lunch, lots of raw fish. He drank too much, so I was to do the afternoon drive back to our holiday rental. But the coffee didn't work. I fell asleep at the wheel, right on the motorway.'

'Does this have to do with Trump?' J asks.

'I remember our car, this eggshell-blue Karmann Ghia. And I remember the bumpiness of that road, narrow and cracked and full of potholes. To the right, there was this deep grass, then the blue Adriatic – right there. We're talking August, hardly any other traffic on the road. But I nodded off, just a few seconds, then woke and righted the car, telling myself, "George! Do *not* do that again!" Suddenly I was waking a second time. The car is out of control. And I see: a woman is in the grass, right where our car is headed. She's waving hard, a black woman, which was not a sight you saw often in Italy then. My boyfriend is sleeping still, his head jiggling. The woman realizes I'm out of control, so she darts on to the tarmac itself. Only, I'm swerving back myself – we're like two people who can't get around each other in a doorway, only at forty miles an hour. I veer away, into the oncoming lane, but now there's a truck coming at me. I think: I'm not dying for this stranger.

So I turn back, driving right at her. She jumps away, but I clip her.

'Total quiet on the road. Or it seemed that way, till I realize my boyfriend is screaming at me. He's asking why I stopped so fast. He must've slept through it. I check the rear-view. No sign of anyone, just the truck that was coming at me. It's stopped – then drives away. Only us now, on this empty stretch of road. I get out, scanning everywhere. My boyfriend asks what in hell I'm doing. I rush into the grass, searching like mad. Nobody. The point of impact was way back, though. Where? I can't tell. A car comes up behind ours, the driver beeping his horn. He zips around, shouting, "*Vaffanculo!*" at my boyfriend, who's still in the car, shrieking at me out the window, because I took the keys and he can't move us to safety. I hold still, there in the tall grass, squinting around me. Trying to see her. Nothing. I run back, get into the driver's seat. "What were you *doing?!*" he asks. I say: "I don't know." Since then, I've so often thought of that – how you can lie without planning to? It's as if there's a liar in you, and you need to block him all the time, and if you don't, he takes control. So I drive away, watching the side of the road as we whoosh along. No black skin, no blood.

'It's a bad night between my boyfriend and me. Not because of what happened; we never speak of it. We just argue about service in the restaurant. He accuses me of being rude to our waiter. Matters improve with sex, but we end the trip with the sense it was *not* a great occasion. When I'm back in Manhattan, my husband asks: "So, was she all right?" And I say, "Yes, yes – much better."'

'Wait, what?' Sindy says. 'I thought you were on vacation with your boyfriend. How'd you have a boyfriend and a husband?'

'Oh, you dear innocent lamb,' Andy says.

'That was my first husband. Not Roger.'

'George,' my current betrothed breaks in, 'with all due respect, this is a very disturbing story. Everyone's already stressed about the results. Could we leave this for now?'

But I go on. 'My husband *at the time*, he tells me, "You

sure got a bit of sun, Georgina!" I say, "Did I, darling? Darn it." He goes, "Not the worst thing." And I kiss him.'

'Technically,' Enson says, '*is* there a way back?'

'If she wins everything else, yes,' Kiara says.

Sindy: 'California has a ton of electoral votes, right?'

J: 'I think those are already included in the projections.'

Beneath a cushion, Roger clasps my wrist, too tightly. I make not the slightest expression of pain. He leans close, whispers, 'Stop it, George.'

Emma bursts into the room. 'Good news!'

Everyone begs for it.

'California and Massachusetts voted to legalize recreational pot.'

'You're killing us, Emma.'

Lucio and his team discreetly ask if everyone enjoyed the service tonight. Our guests mumble distracted thanks, and the Salvadorans clear up.

Amid the tinkle of cutlery and stacked plates, I resume. 'Back in New York, I kept thinking about this woman. I wasn't sure it had happened. But if it didn't, where'd this image of her face come from? Was I half asleep and dreaming? I didn't have a clue who in Italy to contact. I couldn't speak the language, nor was I inclined to involve myself with their police. I didn't even know where it had occurred – a coastal road somewhere between Brindisi and Bari? Where would I even send them to look? And if they found a body? We had continued our vacation, three days more. How would I justify that?'

'Oh, I'm *sure* it was your imagination,' Sindy insists, because it's the polite thing to say. 'No *way* you did anything like that. I know you, Georgie.'

'You don't, actually.'

'We *will* get through this,' David says, back from the den, rambling about the strength of the US Constitution. 'Our republic was built to last.'

'But sadly,' Kiara says, 'our babysitter was not. We should get going. I feel so grim right now. I feel *frightened*. Guys? Can I get hugs?'

David reminds everyone that tomorrow is another day. The elevator outside bings. They're gone.

Emma reports that Trump just won Wisconsin, and CNN is saying Pennsylvania looks bleak.

'But Obama was in Philly campaigning with her *yesterday*! How can she lose Pennsylvania? Bernie wudda won it. He wudda.'

Someone touches my knee. 'And so?' Andy says. 'You broke up with the boyfriend?'

'Not this again!' Roger says, laughing inauthentically. 'Do we really need to hear this right now?'

'Yes, we do,' I say. 'My boyfriend tried to talk me out of it then, too — out of ending our relationship after the Italy trip. We spoke in a very civilized manner. I respected him for taking the break-up so well. Then, suddenly, he became outraged, unused to *ever* not getting his way. He said, "Look, Georgina, if we break up, who am I going to talk about *us* with?" I bristled at that — was he threatening to tell my husband? "We had lovely times," I said. "Those times don't vanish because we're apart." He told me: "They do. They vanish." I shook my head, told him, "Nothing vanishes." He looked at me hard, saying, "That woman did."' I turn toward my husband. 'Remember saying that, Roger?'

'Apparently,' Vanessa says, back from the den, 'Hillary is too distraught to even address supporters. How did my country do this? For the first time, I feel ashamed to be an American.'

Enson and Sindy say their despondent goodbyes. 'We've got an early start tomorrow,' he says. 'Hanging ourselves at dawn.'

The front door opens, closes.

J is gibbering again: 'Because I'm thinking, screw Canada. Can't I, like, move to the multiverse?'

'This election might be done,' Vanessa says pluckily, 'but, you guys, we need to organize now. Block this every step of the way. You with me?'

Emma trots in, saying CNN reports that Clinton called Trump to concede, and he'll be delivering his victory speech soon. Vanessa refuses to watch him gloat, so she summons an Uber, and is gone.

To the last few stragglers – just Andy Rosner, J Vincent

and me in the room now – Roger utters pieties about how people across this country felt left out, that they worked hard but haven't been getting their due. 'Mainstream politicians weren't listening.'

'Are you endorsing Trump now?' Andy says.

'God, no! I'm just trying to make sense of this. These *are* our fellow Americans.'

J – who showed little intensity all night – has a mini-freakout. 'Oh, please. That's the ultimate liberal response: "It's *our* fault." No, actually, it's not! Why do we have to get all understanding about Trump voters? Can't we just say that a bunch of our fellow Americans are godawful? They seriously think women are a bunch of uppity bitches, and blacks are these thievin' lazy negroes – not Barack, though, because he's part of the Oprah club, right? Mexicans are greasy rapist drug dealers, and America was better back when you had segregation. Back when you could still beat up the weirdos.'

'No, you have a point,' Roger says, a hint of Swiss-German-French accent slipping through, as happens when he's furious. 'You hit the nail on the head there.'

'So,' Andy asks my husband, 'you guys mowed down some black lady with your car, and hightailed it?'

How Roger guffaws! He denies that *any* of this happened. We certainly took a trip to Italy early in our love story, but I don't remember *that*. Definitely the sort of event you recall. 'It's my wife's attempt to join the post-truth era!'

'We hit that woman. And we drove away.'

'Nonsense!'

'I should probably go,' J says. The front door opens and closes.

I sit in place, feeling around for a glass of anything, trembling. I'm going to be sick.

Roger's daughter, Scout, finally makes an appearance. 'Hey, I wanted to thank you guys,' she says, meaning her father. 'Thanks from my generation to yours. You've officially ruined the future. Part one: destroy the planet. Part two: wreck the economy. Part three: give nuclear codes to a homophobic racist misogynist with a yellow comb-over. Thank you.'

'It's not *our* doing, Scoutie.'

'Well, it wasn't the young who voted for Trump.'

'Neither did any of us.'

'You *said* Hillary was gonna win this, Dad.'

'You mustn't trust your elders, Scoutie. I'm sorry.'

'Scout,' I say. 'I'm glad you came in. I was telling everyone a story about your dad and me in Italy, and—'

'Stop it, George.'

'Stop what, Dad?'

'These aren't real things she's saying.' He adds confidingly to his daughter: 'You know how she is. It's that.'

'It's *what?*' I shout. '"You know how she is"? Meaning? Not all there anymore? Not the same?'

'You *are* the same,' he responds measuredly. 'That is not what I meant.'

'Isn't it? Isn't that exactly what you're saying? Always?' I'm standing, wobbly, sweat trickling from my armpit, bra strap too tight. I can't get a clear breath. 'Isn't that your point? Roger?'

Someone steadies me. I shake them off, inadvertently knocking a glass, which smashes. Nobody's collecting the shards.

'I seriously cannot deal right now,' Scout says, and stomps out to rejoin Emma in front of the TV.

Roger, too, departs for the Trump speech.

And so I stand there, trying to breathe. I reach for my scalp, wanting a clump of long hair, finding only shorn locks. 'Who's here?' I say, voice shaking. 'Anyone in this room?'

'Me.'

'What are you doing, Andy?'

'Just tweeting how you and Roger murdered a black woman in Italy – you don't mind if I tweet that, right?'

I murmur, 'It's not true.'

'Actually, this'd be *the* perfect time to admit to murder on Twitter. Nobody would care. I should do it as a test.'

'This isn't where I should be.'

'It ain't my country anymore either.'

Down the hall come televised chants of Trump supporters: 'USA! USA! USA!' Their hero thanks the crowd.

'You do realize,' Andy says, 'that *we* were the basket of deplorables?'

Urgently, I break in: 'Andy, would you kiss me? Not saying you should. Just want to know. If you would. Andy? ... Andy?'

TV audio of the victory speech drifts in. 'I've gotten to know our country so well. Tremendous potential. It's gonna be a beautiful thing,' Trump is saying. 'Every single American will have the opportunity to realize his or her fullest potential.'

'Andy? ... Are you there?'

Is anyone left? Anyone here still? Or is it only me and Roger now? Is he back in the living room, standing opposite me, staring? Because I *will not go*. I refuse.

An eerie feeling overcomes me. As if I'd already died – as if, when I fell last year, the brain bleed killed me there and then. Maybe that's why people don't hear me anymore, why they barely respond.

'Roger?' I say. 'Is that you? Are you looking at me?'

I can't see you anymore. But you can't see me either. Just your reflection, bounced back in my dark glasses.

2

Truth is for Losers

My brother's plane plunged into a jungle in central Congo. They'll never find the body, and he won't be coming back. Which is such great news with everything going on in the world lately.

Cheerfully, I slosh milk from a plastic gallon jug into the metal pitcher, poke in my espresso-machine wand, pull down the handle to aerate, then wipe off with a sanitized cloth. 'BARBARA!' I shout across the Starbucks, smiling at the fine citizens awaiting their beverage of choice. 'Tall latte, full fat, extra whip!'

Barbara — like me, a fortyish full-fat Americano, more grande than tall — inspects the side of the cup. 'Uhm, this has "Fleming" written on it?'

I face-palm, and wipe my hand across the green apron. Fleming is my brother's name, and he won't leave my head today. Arranging the memorial has fallen to me, and I'm pretty conflicted. You see, Mom had two sons: first Fleming, then yours truly. He was her favorite, so she's in tatters at the loss, and is yearning to be among others equally devoted to her boy. One problem: at this commemoration thing, it'll be just me and Mom, plus empty seats as far as you can see.

I couldn't stand Fleming, and nor could anybody else. Only our mother — as kind a person as you can imagine — is unaware what a wretched human she delivered. After his decades of deception, she's finally about to learn about her first-born. I can't decide whether to dread this, or long for it.

I have never dared expose my big brother. Not even when we were kids, and Mom left to nurse on the graveyard shift at Bronson Methodist and he'd huck darts at me – I'm talking steel-tipped – Fleming chasing me up the stairs, trying for a 'butt's-eye', as he called a direct strike into my rear. Besides darts, he employed subtler tortures: dismembering my favorite toys, inducing sleep deprivation, filling my bed with frozen fish. I'd slide under the covers, only for my wiggling toes to connect with thawing haddock face. In ninth grade, when I finally had the guts to talk with my unrequited crush, Wendy Farber-Fritsch, he sneaked up and put me in a police choke-hold, cutting off blood to my carotid. My eyes bugged as I faded from consciousness, yet even then I was mouthing an excuse: 'It's okay! He's my br—' I woke, naked and chained to the baseball backstop in a crucifix position. A crowd had formed. Keep in mind I was fourteen with a weight problem. The janitors couldn't locate the bolt cutters, so someone had to drape a fire blanket over me. It kept slipping off, unleashing fresh bursts of hilarity from my audience. Even then, I didn't tell on him. Mom would be leaving for work that night, too, and it'd be just me and Fleming. I couldn't risk it.

The most frightening sight of my childhood was that blank expression on his face as he scanned a room – then stopped on me.

Until – hallelujah! – he was gone, off to college at Michigan, Ann Arbor. Fleming was excellent at school, while I was the dummy, diagnosed with dyslexia much too late. Also, Fleming was effortlessly trim, while I've seen 306 pounds on the scales, though I'm not quite that big today. Anyhow, Fleming departed to conquer the globe, while I stuck around here in Kalamazoo, too ashamed to go outside some days. Eventually, I found work taking portrait photos at the mall. Next, I got hired at the supermarket bakery. I was a stocker at Walmart. Until, at last, I found my calling: boutique beverage curation.

We're a solid crew at this Starbucks, led by our hard-ass store manager, Belinda, with whom I'm secretly and not so secretly in love. There's also my shift supervisor, Uday, a jokester from India mostly raised here in Michigan; also, my fellow star barista, Shey, a Filipina in cherry-red lipstick, born male but transitioning; and her boyfriend,

Greg, a deejay in exile from deepest Mississippi. Belinda keeps pushing me to seek promotion, but I cling to the lowly barista rung – my joy is the non-stop, high-speed, detail-oriented, customer-based servitude, a ton of en-abling, catering to, and generally making customers into entitled freaks. But they paid six bucks for their drink, so hey!

A while back, I worked alongside an older guy, Marty Schlesinger, who'd spent four decades baggage-handling at the airport before signing on as a barista. I tried to protect him despite his snarly moods, hostility to queer staff, and vocal admiration for Mr. Donald J. Trump, who was merely another Republican candidate trailing Ben Carson back then, not our you-*must*-be-kidding president-elect. And I felt sorry for Marty – more than once, I witnessed teen shift supervisors taking him to the carpet for putting his hands in apron pockets, or failing to bus tables, or 'acting disobedient'. When Belinda let Marty go, I wondered if we'd see him again with an assault rifle. If you're listening, Marty: I always tried to be nice to you!

As for me? At the advanced age of forty-two years, I prefer to perform my chores with excellence than to face reprimands from adolescents. If a co-worker prefers to check her cellphone sixty million times after a fight with her boyfriend, I won't bug her. I'll clean the toilets, restock the teas, fill carafes when we get hammered with frap orders. And, for the most part, we at this branch are a team: all loud voices, hard work, and camaraderie. We're the theater kids who grew up and don't have rehearsal anymore. What unites us is *not* being mean — we've got relatives for that, bullies who stomped us into this shape.

I've only begun recounting my own familial bully. After college, Fleming got his MBA at Wharton, intending to become a billionaire entrepreneur. Since he lacked any ideas of his own, he set about stealing someone else's, and persuaded a family firm that leased airplanes in poor countries to hire him as a management consultant. Within a year, he'd fired the founders, and taken total control. On his rare visits home, Fleming always bragged to Mom about how everyone at his work worshipped him, how he had this talent for always making the right call, how much more far-sighted he was than his competitors, how people would kill to work under him, especially the ladies. Once Mom had gone contentedly to bed, Fleming dragged out the tales of debauchery for me: the hot assistants he'd laid, then laid off; the acts of bribery around the Third World; how, for tax reasons, he lived nowhere anymore, moving from luxury to luxury in Dubai, Singapore, London, New York. By that time, he was in his phase of eating only meat, raw Wagyu beef that he sliced into carpaccios with a ten-thousand-dollar Japanese knife – preferably, he informed me, while the latest girlfriend plucked his eyebrows or, when it became the fashion, trimmed his bikini area.

Over the years, his business expanded, with offshore shell companies, an empty villa in the Caymans, sketchy visits to North Korea and Eritrea and Libya, where he once shot a solid-gold Kalashnikov at a flock of gazelles. Proudly, he mentioned that a US grand jury had been looking into his business.

My sole satisfaction was that, during the twenty-odd years since he left home, he'd become gray-skinned, balding, jowly. Fleming, who always taunted me for my looks and weight, had become fat, too. Maddeningly, he seemed pleased about it, as if *his* girth were earned and manly.

When stopping in Kalamazoo, Fleming spurned everyone he knew from schooldays, even supposed best friends. Those who'd remained in town, he said, were losers: stuck here because they couldn't make it anywhere serious. 'Does that include me?' I asked.

'You, Glen? You are definitely a loser.'

Still, I wanted him to like me. Each time he was in town, I regressed: taking his insults, chuckling along – and fighting back the tears when he prodded my tenderest wounds, which Fleming always identified immediately.

Hence my satisfaction in raising this Sharpie and striking 'Fleming' off this Starbucks cup. Over the top, I write 'Barbara', and return the drink to her.

'Uhm, actually?' she says. 'Not *super* wild about a cup that's had someone else's name written on it?'

'I'm here to please!' I say. 'A redo is on its way, lickety-split.' With which I dump the offending latte down the drain.

I ought to dump the memory of Fleming too – let Mom know how her wonderful son *really* was. So, after work, I head to her house.

I find her staring at the kitchen floor. She looks up, tries to smile, can't. Mom got so old.

'What you thinking?' I ask.

'It's stupid.'

'I *only* think stupid things. Never stopped me talking.'

'It's really dumb, Glen.' She pauses. 'Just that I *had* my life. I had my fair share. I know it's goofy. Just wish *I* could've died instead. Why wasn't it me in that plane?'

'For one, you don't fly over Congo that often.' I shouldn't have said that. As you can see, I've got a sarcastic side. But she's too distracted to mind. What troubles her is that, without us having the body to bury, Fleming might not get to heaven.

'Honestly, Mom? I'm not sure that'll be the deciding factor.'

She makes coffee, gazing at the accumulated dirty dishes. Gently, I shift her aside, and clean up. I came over here to cancel this memorial outrage. But I keep scrubbing crockery, then find myself back at my own apartment, compiling a list of everyone in town who knew Fleming. I send out a group email that night. Few people answer, just a handful specifying that they will not attend but *will* celebrate the news in private. After days of this, I'm again opposite Mom in her kitchen, she covering her eyes with one hand, me holding her other, both liver-spotted, knobbled from decades of labor, the palms dry and peeling, which began mysteriously at the hospital on those overnights, which she requested in order to be here for every breakfast, to drive us to school, sleeping while we studied (or were chained to baseball backstops). Always, she picked us up, thrilling over Fleming's larks in the playground, his sporting triumphs, his top grades, and lies about schoolboy heroics. From her own alcoholic father, Mom learned to perceive goodness in men who had none. Which also explains the Finnish guy who studied aviation at WMU and with whom she fell in love, and had us two kids. He just returned to Helsinki, never even writing.

So Mom took care of everything. And, as with all extremely kind people, she leaves me wondering if I'm really seeing everything. Sometimes, I overheard her opening up to Fleming when I was out of the room. Perhaps because he's older, and they grew up together. She dabs her eyes, then reaches over, touches my forehead.

Later that night, I'm lying beside the store manager, Belinda, bedsheets up to our throats, a tub of Ben & Jerry's between our naked bodies. We're on-again, off-again – she flicking it off every few months, me hovering around the on-switch. It's also Belinda who keeps restarting, typically after a partner meeting. These are either uptight occasions, full of diktats to the staff to sell sell sell and clean clean clean, or they're free-for-alls of hellish-customer anecdotes that end with us two, plus Uday, Shey and Greg bar-hopping, dancing and doing karaoke until Belinda is drunk enough to whisper, 'You and me are, like, the only grown-ups in this place.' We make our exit, each taking our own cars, me following to her apartment, to her bed, to her Ben & Jerry's.

At the base of the king-size bed is a flatscreen, playing *Saturday Night Live*, Alec Baldwin impersonating our soon-to-be leader at his first press conference since the election, where he denied paying Russian hookers to pee in front of him. Yes, that actually happened. 'Can you *imagine*,' Belinda says, 'how frickin' mad Donald Trump must be if he's watching right now?'

'Pissed off, but not pissed on,' I joke, glancing at Belinda for approval, trying not to fall for her again, adding: 'Yeah, he must be seething!' Inwardly, I'm doubtful. I mean, did Jon Stewart's *Daily Show* diatribes change anything? Our side lost. And the best fightback we've got, it seems, is a stern teasing on late-night, Alec Baldwin hamming it up through another unfunny *SNL* skit. You remember when Obama said his election showed how 'the arc of history bends toward justice'? But is that honestly where America's history is bending? More a boomerang of history, where we keep throwing out the bad bits, and they keep flying back, hitting us in the mouth.

Sorry – I'm getting snarky. At least I have a dead Fleming to lift my mood. Then I remember the memorial, and slump.

'You should just fake it,' Belinda says, reaching for the ice-cream tub with a telescopic spoon that I bought her as a joke four years ago. (Yes, we have been confused for that long.) 'Seriously, Glen. Just hire impersonators.'

'What, fake mourners? Nice.'

'No, really! This is how you do it,' Belinda says, ever the organizer. 'You get actors to play the scene. Your mom will never know. Who, at a funeral, would think the others are paid shills? Right? You gotta do this, Glen!'

'What my brother deserves is nobody.'

'But does your mom?'

Now, before you condemn this as nuts, understand that I *do* have a finger in the theatrical world. You know me only as a barista, but my passion is the stage. As a young guy, I dreamed of strutting the boards, holding up poor Yorick's skull, swashing buckles. Physically, maybe I'd have ended up as Chubby Friend, or Chubby Villain, or Chubby Funny Man. I never did find out because, throughout school, I kept signing up for theater, and Fleming kept crossing my name off, enrolling me in girls' volleyball. By the time he left for college, I couldn't break into the acting clique. Thankfully, opportunities abounded off stage, which is where I've remained. To this day, I'm a volunteer usher for the Kalamazoo Civic Players. And, in secret, I've spent years plotting out a science-fiction play, in which this law student discovers an online portal that reveals the way everyone is going to die – only she can't save them in time. Not sure what the pay-off is. But my play does raise a serious question: why isn't there more sci-fi in the theater?

My greatest achievement, however, came online, as a contributing reviewer for the *American Standard*. The guy who runs the site, known to me only via email as 'Volkoff1488', lets me post whatever I like. Which led to my triumph, being quoted in a tiny ad in the *New York*

Times arts pages: 'ACHINGLY HUMAN'. That's how I described *Purgatory!*, the knockout Broadway musical adaptation of Dante's hit poem. Admittedly, the ad only quoted me because every major source hated the show. I cite *Variety*: 'So ham-fisted that audiences may imagine that the Dark Prince himself green-lit this production, except *Purgatory!* lacks any of the panache Beelzebub brings to his other work.'

As I top-load beans into the Mastrena coffeemaker, I often think of the *Purgatory!* playwright, Enson Carthy, with whom I have this connection. I imagine us becoming friends.

Most of my reviews, however, are Michigan area, putting me in contact with regional luminaries – and it's this that Belinda is alluding to, saying I should persuade some local acting troupe to do real-life improv for an audience of one: my mother.

'Even if she figures it out, so what? She finds that her eldest son was a complete asshole. You can't lose on this.'

A shudder of excitement passes through me: Glen Pilczuk, directing theater. If I *am* caught, Mom learns that I wanted to protect her, that I always would. Maybe we end up closer, as I wish we were. Because one cost of protecting Fleming all these years is Mom doesn't know *me* either.

I won't dwell on sadness here, especially while I'm buzzing just to ponder venues and actors. They can't hail from Kalamazoo, in case Mom later bumps into them at a store. Not long ago, I had dinner with Jeremiah Mackintosh, founder of *the* top method-acting school in Grand Rapids. I gave his production of *Waiting for Godot* five stars, mainly because he is scary and paid for my meal. What about calling him?

Belinda's telescopic spoon hits bottom on the Chunky Monkey. She's giving me that look: time to head on home? So I do, less wounded than normal because of the ideas pinballing around in my head. What if I pull this off? In jubilation, I punch the air.

Back home, I track down a number for the Mackintosh

acting school, intending to leave a message on voicemail. However, the maestro himself responds, though it's past midnight. After apologizing for the hour, I explain my intent, that I'm picturing something between improv and performance art.

'And how'll we be taken care of?'

'I was gonna offer coach transportation to the venue. For snacks, are you guys cool with Starbucks wraps and cheese-fruit platters?'

'No, how will we be taken *care* of?' he repeats. 'Money. MUN-NEE.'

I sputter out an offer of five hundred dollars, in exchange for thirty actors in non-stop bereavement for a full two hours. They must provide their own mourning costumes, and formulate backstories on how they knew Fleming. To assist, I will provide a bio of my brother. And we have a deal.

I put down the phone, my neck itchy, heart kicking faster than I like for a guy my size. But, as a famed actor once remarked, 'Pressure is a privilege.' Or wait — was that a tennis player? Oh man, what am I doing? I call Mackintosh to cancel. The phone just rings.

The next morning, I wake in full panic. Belinda seduced me into this. I have got to back out. Yet when I tell her at work of my talk with Mackintosh, she's so impressed. 'You're actually doing this!' She dismisses my inability to afford a chapel or rent a theater. 'Have you even *tried* community sports centers?' She ducks into her office to place calls on my behalf. By afternoon, she has the memorial venue: a martial arts academy off I-94 whose sensei has agreed to rent the space for two hours on Saturday, including his sound system and chairs, which his staff will lay out.

I feel I'm going to be sick — yet I want to go on. This must be what stage fright is like. For encouragement, I remind myself that this is deeply dishonest, itself a fitting tribute to Fleming. Except he'd never go to such lengths. If *I* had died in, say, a Pumpkin Spice Latte-related catastrophe, he'd be telling Mom right now that I wasn't a loss, and what's the point of a memorial anyway?

Owing to my jitters, I find the orders piling up. We're running out of vanilla syrup, and a store cleaning is long overdue. I dart out to fill napkin holders and, purely from nerves, knock stir sticks across the floor. Once home, I email Mackintosh a few pages of background on the life of Fleming Pilczuk, all lies – how, with no father around, my big bro always looked out for me. Yes, it's another of my five-star reviews. I can't seem to pan anyone. In the process of writing this alternative brother, I almost miss that person, the Fleming who never lived but will be buried. Through days of preparation, my insides are aflutter, as if I've been downing twenty-shot espressos.

And then, Saturday is here – the kind of morning where your body knows better than your brain: do *not* get out from under the covers. I'm too anxious to shower, so just pull on the borrowed suit, aghast to realize that it's both food-stained and as pungent as an Indian spice cupboard. Uday's uncle, Mr. Shastri, was the only person anyone at work knew who was fat and also owned a suit. Distressingly, I discover that, in addition to spilling curry all over his fine apparel, Mr. Shastri is also less corpulent than myself. The fly won't close, leaving a little triangle of Old Navy boxers peeking out. To conceal this, I attempt to button the suit jacket. It won't close. What if my trousers fall down during the ceremony? It's the sort of brotherly mortification Fleming would adore. I can hear him laughing. Only when I step outside the apartment do I notice that a dazzle is coming off me. The suit isn't gray, as it appeared in Starbucks. It's disco-ball silver.

I pick up Mom, who gives a perplexed frown at my outfit, saying nothing. She is immaculate: church tweed, hair coiffed, face powdered, a thin red band for lips, black liner around those downturned Ukrainian eyes, which were sad slits even in photos from her infancy. But when thinking of Mom, I still see her as the thirty-something nurse who raised us: my mother jogging across a ward, Dixie cup of pain meds in hand, doing blood-pressure checks at 4 a.m., clasping dying hands through the predawn anxiety attacks – then home to two squabbling sons who never even considered what she'd done all night. Every time Mom and I meet nowadays, I think: Someday, you won't be here.

I drive us to the strip-mall parking lot, which is eerily quiet. My stomach gurgles. I couldn't take food or drink this morning, not even a coffee.

'This is a *perfect* little spot.' Mom is never negative. 'What do you think "KTFO" means?' she asks, pointing at the awning over the martial arts gym. We approach the glass entrance door, which is plastered with stickers for fight gear and power-lifting supplements. Her reading glasses come out. 'Well,' she says, squinting, 'it says here that "KTFO" stands for "Knocked the Fuck Out". Gosh! How dedicated!'

I unlock, and flick on the overhead fluorescents. The owner did not, as promised, set up chairs. It's blue gym mats all the way to the octagonal fight cage at the back. The walls are lined with kettlebells and punching bags. The cage entrance is strewn with discarded handwraps. Whiffs of dude-sweat invade our nostrils.

I myself am dripping from the humidity and the worry.

77

When I get apoplectic about the missing chairs, Mom insists that sitting on the floor will bring everyone closer. 'Do you know when his friends should start arriving?'

I check my watch. They should be here already. Still obsessing about chairs, I find a single fold-out seat, and yelp as if it were a gold rush. I open it for Mom, setting it in the center of the mats.

'Very comfortable,' she assures me. 'I should get one like this for home.'

I'm pacing, staring at my watch. For days, I've been emailing Mackintosh. He hasn't responded once. Is he standing me up? Is this it, just me and Mom after all?

'So, Glen, do you know lots of the people who'll be celebrating Flemy with us today?'

Leaning against the wall, I try to work up a confession. Inadvertently, my arm bumps a speedbag, which swings back and tonks me in the jaw. Gasping, I clutch my face, dodging as the punching bag comes in for another swing at me. Why did I listen to Belinda? She isn't even attending today. I have to come clean.

A hissing comes from outside: the hydraulic door of a coach. Voices sound in the parking lot. 'Wait here, Mom.' I hustle out, realizing that the only thing worse than them *not* showing is this. I have my mourners, and I want to run.

The coach is parked diagonally across four spaces, disgorging thespians, a few doing vocal exercises, others gossiping about auditions, a few stretching. It only then occurs to me: how can I explain that *all* the mourners – supposedly with no connection to one other – arrived on the same coach? And the gym door is glass, so Mom can see this. I position myself to block her view. Should I have the actors enter gradually? Mackintosh himself stumbles down the bus stairs, and I wave him over, saying we must hurry – I only have two hours here! Wasn't everyone supposed to come in funeral clothes? Not drainpipe jogging pants, Nikes, hoodies.

'Friars in Shakespearean times often wore hooded vestments,' Mackintosh reminds me, slurring.

'This isn't a Shakespearean scene. This is present day. I thought I was clear in my emails.'

'Yes, yes, yes,' he responds impatiently. 'Wait – what emails?'

'I sent you millions of emails! About my brother's life. About the dress code.'

'You can't expect me to read *millions* of emails.'

'But you will be master of ceremonies, right? As I specified.'

In a huff, Mackintosh submits, but clearly has nothing prepared. Also, he seems fairly drunk. The gym door opens behind me. My mother stands there, looking around. She touches her chest, moved that this many people have come. 'Thank you so much, everyone. Won't you all join me inside?'

She takes my arm, whispering, 'His friends were all so *young.*'

And she's right: I paid Mackintosh for a troupe of professionals, but these are nearly all in their early twenties, posing as friends of a man who died at forty-five. The last time Fleming spent a full summer in Kalamazoo, these kids were probably four years old. A few clutch each other by the shoulders, saying things like: 'He's gone, Taylor, and we've just got to come to terms with that.'

A skinny Arab-American in a black dress shirt (at least *he* dressed for the occasion) falls to his knees in the parking lot, and pulls at his collar, as if to tear it. My mother hastens back, helping the young man to his feet.

He pushes her away. 'You don't get it, lady! You don't have any idea what he meant to me!'

'Oh, I am so sorry, dear. How did you know my son?'

At this, he blanches, not having realized this was the mother. 'Ohmigod, I'm so sorry. I was just. I was. I ...'

I shout at them: 'Everyone inside!'

As I hold the entrance door open, I keep looking over at my parked little Mazda, tempted to burn out of here. I can't stop sweating. What is this suit made of? Everyone trudges somberly into Knocked the Fuck Out, the actors settling in small groups on the blue mats, fake-crying, real-hugging – and turning away at the approach of Mom, as if she keeps breaking the fourth wall.

I lead her to the lone fold-out chair, and Mackintosh takes his place before us.

'Listen up, guys!' he shouts, clapping twice. 'Okay, so Fleming Pilzook? This was a real special one. But you know that.' He takes a tipsy stumble, stifles a burp, and regains his balance. 'Fleming was one of us. He loved the outdoors. And he loved bowling. As a surfer, he explored the beaches of Southern California.'

A few audience members cheer in recognition. I know these lines, too. What are they again? Then I've got it: the eulogy scene from *The Big Lebowski*.

Mom whispers to me: 'I never knew Flemy bowled or surfed.'

'He died,' Mackintosh continues, 'like so many young men of his generation, before his time. In your wisdom, Lord, you took him!' With this, he thrusts his arm upward, not toward the heavens but pointing at fluorescent lights. Blinded, he falls sideways on to the mats.

I hurry over, pulling him upright.

'I'm fine, for crying out loud!' He shoves me off,

muttering, 'I blocked it out that way.' He proceeds to the gym boom box, speaking of a song that meant a great deal to Fleming. Mackintosh seems to realize only upon reaching the CD lid that he didn't bring any music. He looks around, drowning. My sweaty trouser legs are pressed together in the skin-tight silver suit. But the show goes on, and so does Mackintosh. 'A melody that'll bring us all smiles and, I daresay, a coupla tears. Here goes.' He presses play on whatever happens to be in the boom box CD player, and sweeps back his hair, earnestly awaiting the promised heart-warming song.

Heavy-metal guitar and a ferocious drumbeat rip forth from the speakers – it's 'Master of the Puppets' by Metallica, the lead singer growling demonically until Mackintosh hits stop, looks reflective for an instant, then offers reminiscences of his time puppeteering on Cape Cod.

I notice that mourners keep drifting out the front door, so I speed-tiptoe after them, finding a clutch of actors on smoke break in the parking lot. 'Hey, you guys, sorry,' I say, the fingers of each hand pressed together. 'Uhm, I did actually pay you what is, for me, kind of a lot of money for a couple of hours of grief improv. So, uhm, might it be okay if you guys could possibly resume mourning? Is that cool?'

'Paid us? You didn't pay us. *We* pay to take this class.'

Mackintosh must've dubbed this a school exercise, and pocketed the money.

They flick away their cigarettes. 'But fine. Whatever.'

As I follow the student actors back toward the gym, a Ram truck pulls up beside us, and a thick-shouldered mountain of a guy throws out a duffel bag, jumping down after.

'Oh, hey there,' I say. 'Are you a friend of my brother's?'

He furrows his brow, and barges into the gym, where he hollers inquiries about when the Thai boxing master class begins, and that he's gonna work the heavy bag while he waits.

Mackintosh, seemingly out of material, asks his students, 'Anyone else care to testify?'

The young Arab-American jumps up as if invited on stage by a magician. He spins around before us, his face at odds with itself: the forehead distraught, the lips euphoric. 'Ohmigod, I'm so nervous right now. Was there *ever* anyone like ...' He's forgotten the name. 'Like this guy who sadly passed?'

'Totally not,' someone responds.

'You know how him and me met?'

'You and *Fleming*,' I prompt him.

'Yeah, how me and Flaming met? The sun was pouring down, and I see this guy, Flaming, on the other side of the street. He's walking deaf kids to school.'

Mom gapes at me, whispering, 'Where was *this*?'

'Me and Flaming, we had our battles, sure. But we became like family.' Covering his eyes, the actor chortles. 'Did anybody make you *laugh* like Flaming? Guys?'

The crowd answers with cackles of laughter, each actor turning to the next, improvising supposed recollections of Fleming.

I'm paralytic with embarrassment, trying not to make eye contact with my mother.

A young woman takes her turn, pushing the other actor back to the mat. Wide-eyed, she informs us that words aren't her strong point, so she'll dance. And she does, very badly, repeatedly telling us she doesn't have the right shoes. By the end, it's mainly jazz hands, with the background noise of a cage fighter pounding the heavy bag with kicks.

Mom asks if she might take a break, and I lead her out, where we pass another cauliflower-eared brawler, who's here for the Brazilian jiu-jitsu open practice. Apparently, the sensei never informed his clients of the memorial – and there's no dissuading men whose noses go in three directions. I leave Mom in the parking lot, and rush back inside, intending to pose stern questions about Mackintosh's artistic vision. However, he and his cast are refusing to break character. When I enter, a woman in her thirties – hollow cheeks, long black hair and a men's navy wool coat – is stating her name as if at Alcoholics Anonymous. 'So, like, for those that don't know me, I'm Isabella?'

'Hey, Isabella!'

'This isn't happening right now. He's really gone. I can say it – but I can't *get* it. You know? But Fleming loved all you guys.' She reaches out, like Evita to the masses. I almost expect her to shout, '*And* I'm carrying Fleming's baby!' Instead, she stuffs her hands in her coat pockets, and fake-weeps. In all my years as an online reviewer, including dinner-theater performances of *Phantom of the Opera* on a riverboat, I've rarely encountered lesser portrayals of the deep human emotions.

Meanwhile, my poor mother – having gotten some air outside – is struggling to return, politely stepping aside to let ever more fighters enter. I can't allow her to witness Isabella's display, so hasten toward the performer, my forefinger raised as I lean to her ear. 'Thank you, Isabella, so much for your efforts today. You have a ton of talent. I hope you don't mind taking notes right now. But I *would* invite you to tone it down just a tad? Is that something that you could work with?'

'Excuse me? Your role here is what?'

'Director. Or producer.' Mom is approaching. 'I don't have time to get into this right now. If this isn't working for you, I think you need to leave.'

Isabella flares her nostrils contemptuously, blows a kiss to her peers, and struts past my mother, and out the door.

At this point, the gym contains fewer mourners than martial artists, several rolling on the mats around us, sometimes slamming bodily into the bereaved, who leap aside, squeaking.

Mom gives me a hug, arms as far around me as possible, patting the soaked tail of my untucked dress shirt. 'Fleming never did any of that stuff they said.' She leans back, looking at me.

'I guess people are being nice.'

She gives a skeptical look, then turns sincere. 'I'm going to miss your brother. *So* miss him.'

I hurry my mother through quick goodbyes, and help her into the passenger seat of my car, speeding us away. I have no idea what she thinks just happened. It's always hard to tell how much Mom knows. For heaven's sake, when we were kids, she never even believed Fleming smoked cigarettes! He could've lit up in front of her, and she'd still have denied it. She'll adore her eldest son, and the facts must just fall in line.

After dropping her at the house, I close the car door and exhale, wiping this greasy face of mine, trying not to see myself in the rear-view mirror. My unease about everything won't subside over the next few days. Because I know it now: nothing will change between me and Mom. It never will.

I tidy a chaos of lids, fill the sugar and honey dispensers, quick-sweep the floor, and return behind the coffee machine to the awaiting district manager, offering him a White Chocolate Gingerbread Frappuccino from the secret menu, kowtowing to this superior who's nearly young enough to be a son. He asks if I prefer African coffee beans or the blends. 'Well, I love citrusy everything, and the floral aspect gives depth,' I chirp, mind elsewhere, recalling that I was a theater impresario, as I always wanted – and I wasn't any good. I'm not that guy; I'm this guy. 'As for the aged fermented beans from Southeast Asia added to the Africans – not sure I love that yet. It's spicy but sort of musty tasting. Or is that just me?'

The district manager states that the blend is awesome, so I back down immediately, and excuse myself to take an order from a customer named Brett, who wears a red 'MAKE AMERICA GREAT AGAIN' cap. After merely making his drink great, I offer Brett a peacemaking smile, as if to say: 'We're not on the same side. But we're both reasonable human beings. And I respect you.' I hand over his caramel macchiato, and he snatches it away without acknowledging my existence.

Sometimes, I think the world has become a science-fiction play, where only a few of us can see that there are monsters lurking among us. Those of us who *can* tell – we could wreck ourselves screaming out warnings, putting ourselves in danger by doing so. Or we could submit, and pretend to notice nothing. It's so much safer to stay quiet.

After flirting with Belinda, the district manager bids his farewells, forgetting to include me. Once he's gone, Belinda rolls her eyes about the guy, and helps me do the close, taking care of the register as I ease out the homeless woman camped in an armchair, the spacey students, the meth-head in the toilet. I gather the marked-out food, sneaking sandwiches to the more desperate characters I just ejected.

When I return, Belinda says, 'I didn't see that, didn't hear it,' and she locks the front door, inviting me to her office. I stand up straighter, chin up, heart speeding, trying to taste my breath. We'll be kissing in there.

'Glen, we work in the same store,' she says, flicking on the office light, flicking off our relationship. 'We can't be doing this anymore.'

'I could always quit,' I say, as if joking.

'Can't let you. You're the best barista in Kalamazoo.'

Once back at my apartment, I settle into my La-Z-Boy, swallowing my distress by swallowing Mexi-wraps. I watch my rabbit, Hammerstein, bound around the white shag carpet as if he were leaping a forest of cotton wool. My phone rings, and it's Fleming.

'Good turnout?' he asks, the line hissing.

'Where are you calling from? The underworld?'

'Well, not from any place you've ever been, brother. More than that, you don't need to know.'

I expected this call – he admires himself too much to forgo news of his own memorial. 'Roughly forty people showed,' I report, unsure why I'm exaggerating.

He asks for names, and I claim not to remember, though I describe a few participants.

'I don't recognize *any* of those losers. But there you go – people always remember me, and I never knew they even existed!'

You see after his reported death, the grand jury closed its investigation. That was the upside of dying in a jungle. 'Flem, does Mom know you're still alive? I think she does, right?'

'What Mom knows and what I know aren't your concern, fat boy.'

'But you're *not* coming back.' This was my condition for participating in his vanity project of a memorial.

'There is no way back. Or don't you trust me?'

He orders me to say I'll miss him. I refuse.

'Glen, you know that now I *have* to make you say it.'

In a flare of anger (and with the safety of a long-distance phone line between us), I tell him the truth about this goddamn memorial, that nobody wanted to come, that even his oldest friends didn't respond to the email. 'I had to *pay* people to attend. For Mom's sake. Nobody cares that you died, Flem. Doesn't that upset you at all?'

'You *hired* people?' He bursts into laughter. 'Oh, that is beautiful. You moron.'

'Actors were the only people convincing enough to seem like they gave a damn that you had stopped existing.'

'Don't pretend it was for me. You got to do your adorable little theater production. Am I right?' he says, capable of targeting me instantly.

'You're completely off base. I was being nice to Mom.'

93

'Yeah, right. And so, there wasn't an Isabella there, right?'

'A who?'

'A woman called Isabella never showed?'

I recognize that name: the woman I told to leave. But I don't disclose this yet. 'Sounds like you mind, Fleming. Getting teary now?' He isn't, of course. I've never heard my brother upset. But sometimes I try.

'Do I mind that my girl never showed? Zero.' However, he sounds as close to hurt as I can remember.

'Describe her again?'

He does, and it's her. But I keep asking more details, dragging this out. Partly because I hate to deceive. Partly because, after this conversation, I won't talk again with my brother. On the line right now is the only person who was also present through my childhood, after Dad went, when Mom dated all those terrible guys, when she crashed the car with me in the back and Fleming in front, his head bashing the windshield, and he laughed and laughed, and passed out. Me and him remember that stuff, even if we never talk about it – he, because it doesn't matter; me, because it still matters. The truth is, Fleming knows me better than anyone.

'She never showed,' I tell him. 'You're dead to the world. Now get off my phone.'

'Bye, brother.'

'Bye, brother.' I hesitate. 'Actually – wait!'

But he already hung up. And I don't know which of us won.

3
Leakzilla

THE BIGGEST SCANDAL IN history was inevitable in retrospect. Hackers breached all the main email providers – Gmail, Yahoo, Hotmail, iCloud, everything – and downloaded each personal message ever archived, posting the whole lot online. For a while, the authorities battled to take it down. But the data dump kept appearing elsewhere. Log on to any of the mirrored sites, type in a name, and you could pore over the most intimate emails, be they from Bob Dylan or Kellyanne Conway or the Queen.

Governments were the first casualty. Politicians, it turned out, are not always engaged in wicked conspiracy. More often, they're plain bunglers. As an infamous email read: 'Could one of you guys please show Hillary how to shut down Windows? Not kidding. She seriously doesn't know.'

Above all, Leakzilla achieved what nobody believed possible: it almost overshadowed the craziness of those first years of the Trump presidency – the shallow cruelties and the dunderhead incompetence, the allies snubbed and the foes cuddled, the Twitter bombast that tripped into frightening confrontations. But such matters seemed distant indeed when right there online was an email from 2004, where your sister tells her best friend how your husband hit on her *during your wedding*. Now everyone knew, and everyone was pissed. Much of the world was either apologizing, or refusing to. Bank details and home addresses and phone numbers gushed out. Lawsuits followed; divorces, above all.

At first, suspicion turned on Russia, given that Moscow

had so recently won an American election. But Leakzilla included embarrassing emails from top Russian politicians, too, as well as plentiful messages that disgraced Chinese officials. The mischief-makers, whoever they were, had spared nobody.

Some commentators dubbed Leakzilla a welcome flush of honesty, sluicing out the hypocrisy of humankind. Meanwhile scholars appreciated the trove of private correspondence gaining unmatched insight into those who would become noteworthy. Although, as contrarians pointed out, many of the people who *might've* become noteworthy had now been eliminated from contention by public shaming.

A few categories were spared, however: the very young and the very old, because neither had learned email; the uneducated poor, who'd rarely had computer access; and the paranoid, who'd been correct all along. As for millennials, they had already been sharing so much of their intimate lives that few understood what the problem was with this megaleak. A handful of individuals were just lucky. Donald Trump, it turned out, never used email. Nor did Vladimir

Putin. Julian Assange shunned it, too. When an MSNBC host mentioned this coincidence, the president retaliated via tweet. 'Why won't madcow @maddow say WOODY ALLEN never uses email either? Maybe HE was behind #Leakzilla. Dishonest media won't report this. Sad!'

Besides the public fallout, a private cost was paid, too: new romance sputtered. Love proved hard to sustain when its early shine was so readily tarnished by a simple web search: 'Wait, this guy said *that*? I don't care if it was 1999. Who even *says* that?'

To combat this sexless trend, marketers came up with the concept of 'honor dates', whereby each member of a prospective couple vowed never to read the other's past emails. To ensure that 'honor' was also honest, online matchmaking services emerged. You'd set up a profile, swipe right or left, and message-flirt, as per normal. But your true name and identifying features were encrypted until you chose to disclose.

One such honor date is unfolding right now at Jake's Famous Crawfish in Portland, Oregon.

To set the scene: the place is packed tonight, its staff in their old-timey uniforms – white bow ties, white jackets – swooping among the tables like seagulls. Tim Kalogerakis sits in a window booth, looking with affection around the wood-paneled restaurant, where he always brings out-of-town visitors. His date almost counts as that, having only recently moved here for a job. Beyond that fact, he learned little more in their online exchanges besides her mobile number, from which a series of texts now vibrates his smartphone, she apologizing for her lateness, he responding, 'No prob!'

If asked, Tim tells people he recently got out of a long-term relationship, a claim that was truer when he started saying it two years ago. He's been puttering along since, busy with his many jobs and pretty contented, truth be told. If there's a speck of concern, it pertains to the number fifty. He hit that milestone recently. Never married, no kids, but plenty of buddies – albeit fewer than once. Each time a friend stops calling these days, you can't help wondering, 'Was it something I emailed?'

Tim knows that, after fifty, next up is the big Six-Oh —
and that is *old*. Chances of a long-term partner will dwindle
just as need rises, especially if he's ever taken ill, heaven
forbid. Sure, it's mercenary to consider a relationship that
way, but it does enter his thinking. Not long ago, Tim was
making a giant paella at a friend's backyard party, and his
glasses fogged from steam off the bubbling yellow rice,
mussels and chorizo. He mumbled to himself that he'd
better board a train soon or there wouldn't be many more
departures from this station — only to wince, realizing he'd
just compared women to a train schedule. Thank hell, he
thought, that my random dumb reflections can't be hacked
and uploaded for everyone to read!

He glances across the booth, where someone will soon
sit, a designer who just started at Nike, temporarily renting
a studio apartment in Beaverton. She wants advice on cool
neighborhoods in the city. 'I can do that,' he mutters, a
passing waitress pausing, then whipping by.

Tim sips tap water, ice cubes tinkling, and is genuinely
unbothered by his date's tardiness. He's not fretful that

way, a big lumbering fella in Pacific Northwest style, red-and-black-checked flannel lumberjack shirt, dark messy hair lined with threads of silver, black-rimmed glasses, no-name loose jeans, tan work boots. He could belong to a construction crew; he could be a hipster. But he's neither, just himself, and starting from zero tonight, which is so liberating, given how surveilled everyone feels since Leakzilla.

He looks to the doorway again. And there she is, casting around for her date. Tim raises his hand, half standing as he smiles broadly, waving her over.

'I am so, so embarrassed,' she says, one hand contritely against her chest, the other wriggling out of a white, down-padded Nike jacket with fake-fur collar. She flings her handbag up the other side of the booth, and scoots along the banquette after it. 'I am never normally late. I am so sorry.' She'd probably have added his name after that apology, but it's a fact neither is yet allowed. She explains that, having no sense of direction, she must rely on GPS to get anywhere – she'll probably need it to find the washrooms later! But Google Maps just flunked out, sending her to another restaurant also called Jake's – at which point her data topped out, and she was obliged to canvass passers-by, whose street directions meant nothing in this unknown city. 'Complete disaster. Forgive me.'

'Really, no problem,' he assures her. 'I like being kept waiting. It lets me think, which I consider a luxury nowadays, right? Just thinking, doing nothing. Know what I mean?' A crinkly grin rises on his cheeks. Previous girlfriends said he had a lovely smile, so he tries to make it prominent – Tim considers this his version of the push-up bra. Then again, he remembers that women aren't supposed to be as into looks, right? Or maybe I only think that because of patriarchal subjection, or subjugation, or subjectivity, he reckons, struggling to summon a long-ago women's studies course at community college, before he dropped out altogether.

Most of his attention, however, is on how different she looks to her profile photo. On HonrDate, she wasn't anywhere *near* this cute. The photo had her as dark, hair pulled back, a little serious. In life, she wears her hair down, tightly coiled black ringlets, stunning big brown eyes, a sporty but curvaceous physique – other men in the restaurant keep finding excuses to scope her. This is odd for Tim, who never asks out super-attractive women. He prefers someone nice. Which isn't to say pretty and nice are mutually exclusive. But who can deny that plain folk (including himself in this) try harder? So, her unexpected attractiveness makes his spirits drop. Tonight will be a slow-burn failure, as she slowly recognizes he's not at her level. He thinks, I must be the first dude in history to meet an online date and be *disappointed* that she's a hottie. Tim would smile at this, but he dislikes that he thought the word 'hottie' – he prides himself on being respectful of women.

And yet when the app asked 'Preferred Age of Partner', he clicked twenty-five to thirty-five. He felt less piggish that the woman he ended up chatting with was not at the absolute youngest end of that spectrum – we'll even have a few years of music in common, he figured. Plus, what she lacks in years, I can offer back in local knowledge.

Still, their online chat suggested she's hugely accomplished, which intimidates him. And now drop-dead, too? Also, she's not from Portland, so probably won't understand a patchwork career like his.

'Hey, can I offer you a drink?' he says, meaning, 'Can I get one to calm down?' He rambles on about Oregon craft breweries, realizing midway that he has skidded into bore territory, unsure how to reverse out. She's playing along, nodding, smiling. She wants to make friends in Portland, and seems open and patient – even if, he feels, she's already dropped him from the 'has-potential' category.

'My preference would probably be wine, if that's cool with you?' she says. 'Something local, maybe?'

'We can do that.'

'I've actually never gone on an honor date before. Kinda cool, right?'

'I never did *any* online dating. I'm not normally a cutting-edge guy when it comes to trends and computer stuff.' He regrets casting himself as the oldster, yet plods further into that characterization, saying how he just got his first smartphone.

'What kind?'

He has to take it out to check – it was the cheapest they had at T-Mobile, recommended by the teenager working there. Tim looks down his nose at the little screen, seeking a brand name, mumbling, 'This glasses prescription is *not* right.'

'Time for bifocals, maybe. My mom has those. They really help.'

He laughs, shriveling inside. 'It says "ZTE Avid Trio". Is that a good brand? Seems pretty good to me.' He persists in revealing his tech-backwardness, that he's never tried Uber, never seen a Snapchat, has no idea what Slack is, and keeps hearing talk of Tumblr. 'It's for sharing things, right?'

'I think pretty much everything is these days.'

'And what's that program, Pinterest?' Why, Tim asks himself, can't I cut this out? 'There's also that really famous one. What is it, Instamessage?'

She covers her chuckle, looking at him sweetly, big

brown eyes melting Tim. With astonishment, he realizes: she's finding me cute! He grins back, his biggest, best smile.

He asks to hear more about her work, knowing from their messaging that Nike headhunted her, and that she previously worked at the Brooklyn fashion house Sindy Pereira, making her name by creating the hashtag insignia on a hot-selling line of exercise wear for lounging.

'So Nike recruited you to finally come up with a catchy logo, I'm guessing,' he kids, another of his famous smiles.

'Exactly!' she responds, beaming back. 'That swoosh never really caught on, right?' Her unit is part of Nike's innovation kitchen, which concocts limited-edition shoes for middle-aged men obsessive about collecting kicks, some owning hundreds of pairs, never putting them on, just storing them in the original boxes. 'You can find kicks that go for, like, ten grand. I'm not even joking.'

'And by "kicks", you mean …?'

'Oh, excuse me – "kicks" is just a word for sneakers. Yeah, so if you go online? You'll find people trading, like, rare Dunks or retro Jordans or Yeezys for, like, mad cash.

When there's a big Nike release, there are riots. People get killed. It's seriously insane.'

After taking this in, he says, 'And the Nike gig is your dream job?'

'Oh, absolutely.' Her pleasure transitions into narrow-eyed doubt. 'Wait – how did you know this is my dream job? I never told you that.' Nowadays, it's so easy to suspect everyone, that they know the insides of you, that they've read you. 'You *swear* you did not Zilla me?'

'Hey, I don't even know your name! And you didn't Zilla *me*, right?'

'You're sounding kinda nervous,' she jokes, adding, 'You don't want me to find out about the felonies?'

'Hey, the DA's charges never stuck.' Tim is delighted with himself, that he's keeping up.

'Well, it is hard to make a capital case.'

'Ooh, dark humor.'

'No, but honestly,' she resumes, 'what are you?/Who are you?/Fill in the blanks. You said in your messages how you do a bunch of different jobs?'

He lists a few: boat captain to this scientist doing research on salinity in local waterways; paella maker for hire at big parties; property manager (he worked in construction for years, so knows how to maintain a house); small-business consultant; carpenter; and, recently, cider maker and sourdough maker.

'Are you being real right now?'

Seeing that she's amused, he tells of his personal currency, how he prints little denominated bills and gives them to friends around Portland who've done him a solid. They can redeem them for things like a bottle of Tim's cider, or one of his sourdough baguettes, or a Sunday breakfast that he'll come to their home and cook.

'You are so cool,' she says. 'You are officially my first *Portlandia* experience.'

The menus arrive, and he regales her with tales of Jake's, its hundred-and-twenty-five-year history, how Humphrey Bogart ate here. She passes on ordering an appetizer, and this deflates him slightly – would she rather hurry through this? Going straight to the mains, she takes the Dungeness crab and bay shrimp cakes. To be personable, he opts for the same, suggests a bottle of the Ponzi Pinot Gris, from Willamette Valley. 'If you're into desserts, they've got a famous one here: the chocolate bag.'

'Chocolate what?'

'A bag made of chocolate, filled with berries. You'll see.' He keeps trying to amuse her, describing his house next, which is partly held up with wires since a major storm. He was away at the time, and his house-sitter called in the middle of the night, saying: 'Uhm, Tim? You have no roof right now. It's raining in your living room. Right in front of me.'

'What did you do?'

'I told her, "Take the pictures off the walls."'

'You have paintings?'

'Just old stuff my mother had, plus family photos.'

'You sure sound like you're cool under pressure. Sorry – I don't want to sound like I'm evaluating you on everything.'

'No, no – judge away.'

'I *hate* feeling judged. Remember that if I order the chocolate bag!'

He laughs.

'So,' she resumes. 'More about where you're from, your people.'

He takes a glug of water, and tells of his beloved mother, who died in 2004 of ovarian cancer – he hurries past this fact, for his voice still cracks each time he says it aloud. As for Dad, he was a salesman who passed away in Mexico back in the Nineties, having divorced Mom and moved south to write poetry, convinced he was one of the greats. Perhaps because Dad was a conventional success and then dumped it all, wrecking the family in the process, Tim has always avoided the shackles of mainstream living.

'Which is how you ended up in Portland?'

Actually, he was already from Oregon, although he did spend several years living elsewhere around the country, learning the trades. He even had a spell in New York during the bad old days, the late Eighties, waiting tables at Tavern on the Green, he and the other staff rubbing black coffee on their filthy trousers to keep them dark. For a spell, he installed cedar siding around the West Coast, and moved back to Portland when his mother fell ill, eventually taking over her house.

'With her pictures on the wall.'

'Right, exactly. I was glad to be back, though. It's tiring, always moving. But how about you? Have you moved much?' he asks, as if he didn't know.

But Tim is fully aware that she moved throughout her childhood. Indeed, he knows plenty. When they were messaging on HonrDate, she let slip about her previous job, after which he searched the Sindy Pereira website, and found under the 'About Us' section a little bio of its exercise-wear designer, Nelly Haas. With her name, he visited Leakzilla, and spent hours reading her old emails. He knew it was wrong – *the* most fundamental violation of this date. But he was at a disadvantage with her being so much younger and more accomplished. He needed a secret advantage, and he found it.

On her online profile, she had stated under 'Political

Preference: liberal'. But her emails of the past few years charted a growing disillusionment with Barack Obama, which played out in messages to her sister, whose conservative views had gradually swayed Nelly. According to her sister, the then-president had been divisive on race; he'd screwed up international relations; he was self-regarding. As the years passed, Nelly started emailing her own links to Fox News clips, *Wall Street Journal* opinion pieces, scare articles from the *Daily Mail* online and Breitbart, marking them: 'Did you see this??!?' Writing to her sister, Nelly bemoaned her Brooklyn workplace, where everyone was so left wing and, she said, it was impossible to say anything without them jumping down your throat. If she struggled in New York, Tim figured, she'll surely find it challenging in Portland, which is still floating in its Bernie bubble. She must've known that, and dearly wanted friends in this city. So, she ticked 'liberal', just as Tim had. But he knows better now, and this is his secret to her heart: she voted Trump.

'Sorry,' he says. 'I've been blabbing so much about my stupid paellas and whatnot.'

'No, no – that was cool.'

'Could I perhaps hear a bit more about you? You say you didn't grow up in one place?'

'Not at all.' Her father was career military, and moved the family through various bases overseas and back in the homeland. For college, she enrolled at Florida State, then did a year in Japan teaching English, during which she was once drugged and still doesn't know exactly what happened. She took a job in Chicago at a wine shop, which was a huge departure, then studied commercial art and design, got into advertising, and ended up designing hipster exercise wear in Williamsburg, where she would *never* have seen herself. 'I was not a cool kid growing up.'

'Why, are all people in Brooklyn nowadays "the cool kids"?'

'I think they *are*. Or, they're the cool kids, pretending they *aren't* the cool kids. Does that make sense? I don't know. For me, the outdoors was just way too important.'

'To be cool?'

'No, no – the outdoors meaning Brooklyn wasn't for

me. But actually, I kinda feel I need to be more weird to fit in around here.'

'Oh, I'm sure you got some weird in you.' He smiles. 'Must be something. Something secret. Something you don't like to tell.'

'Not really.'

'Oh, come on now!'

'Okay, here's something. My great-grandfather invented prunes. Is that weird?'

'Prunes?! He did not invent prunes!'

'No, he totally did!'

'No frickin way he invented prunes!'

'Who, then? Somebody had to.'

'So since I don't know the inventor's name, we default back to Gramps? Prunes weren't invented two generations ago. They've been around since forever. They're like honey. It's like telling me your grandfather invented honey!'

'My *great*-grandfather.'

'Oh, in *that* case.'

Both of them are giggling now, she nearly losing it, insisting: 'It's true! Honestly! He did!'

The waiter appears, displaying their bottle. Tim invites her to taste, seeing as she worked at a wine shop once.

'Just so there's no confusion,' she says, 'we're going Dutch on this meal.'

'We'll see about that.'

'No, no – that's iron-clad. That's why I'm saying it. Agreed?'

'But this gets me wondering,' he says. 'Is it true about the Dutch? That they're always splitting checks?'

'Actually, I never found any nation that does it as much as us guys. Should be called "going American", right? We like things fair and balanced, wouldn't you—'

'Hey, sorry – can I just say how *well* this is going?'

'Our date? Okay, that was kinda weird,' she says, with a shy smile. 'Portland rules apply, I guess.'

'But you agree?'

She looks at him, eyes gleaming. 'Maybe.'

Has this ever happened? An online date that *works*. Part

of his elation is that they're not droning on about Leakzilla, which seems to be all anyone discusses anymore. We're connecting, like people used to. No? So he risks the next step, nudging their discussion toward politics. 'You know what happened not far from this restaurant? Those anti-Trump riots after the election. Just a few blocks away. And I gotta say,' he adds, giving a knowing look, 'I will never understand why people think it's a good idea to smash windows when they don't get their way.'

'Yeah, I totally do not get needless destruction like that.'

'People around here think of Trump as the devil incarnate,' he goes on, his boldest foray yet, holding her gaze an instant too long, as if to wink, as if to say, You're safe with me.

'"Devil incarnate" is a bit extreme,' she says. 'But, like I put on the profile, I *am* pretty liberal.'

'Well, hey, this being Portland, you gotta tick all the liberal boxes, or they'll lynch you! Won't find many out-of-the-closet Republicans in these parts.' He mentions how his friends were all rabidly against Trump, and how the election result put them either into deep depression or wild rage – those seemed the only options. 'What I can't get my head around,' he says, 'is old Obama. If that guy really knew the election was being hacked by Russian spies, how does he do nothing? And, like, are we sure the Russians did that? And if they did, how significant was it really? Grumbling about the Russians? Kinda sounds like sour grapes, right? And even if it *was* true, the person to criticize is Barack Obama. Like, how asleep at the wheel was that guy?'

'Hey, watch what you say about Barry. He's still my man. Why couldn't we have four more years of him?'

Tim hesitates. She's maintaining her liberal disguise, embarrassed to contradict what she put online. Carefully, he persists, giving her openings to slip to the Right, feeding itsy little Tea Party gambits. She bats them back. Tim starts to worry that he's only worsening her situation – each time she's forced to assert a liberal position, it's harder to backtrack without looking like a fake. If we actually develop a relationship, she could be condemned to impersonate a progressive forever! Unless she already knows nothing will develop, and is only getting through tonight. His heart drops. Am I screwing this up? He takes a long sip of wine. If he joins her in acting like a full-throated liberal, then the most attractive woman he's met in *years* will think he's another Portland bleeding-heart. Yet if he forces her into the open, she'll know he violated the honor-date rules. He cannot play around here; this woman is way smarter than he is. 'But – but don't you sort of think, getting back to Trump for a second, that the reason everyone outside this city and the Northeast chose this president is because people want a leader who's upfront? Love him or hate him, everyone knows that Trump tells it like it is. And people want that.'

'Lots of people would say Trump *doesn't* tell it like it is.'

'Oh, come on – even folk who hate the guy agree that he never pretended he's someone he's not. Problem is, liberals can't deal with a self-made man who comes out and says it. And you've got to agree: people *should* just come out and say stuff more. Right?'

'Wait, did you call Trump self-made? He inherited a ton of money. And how successful is he really? Do we know? He never released his full tax returns, right? All we know is that he lost nine hundred million dollars one year. Now, if it were five hundred million, you could consider that misfortune,' she quips. 'But losing nine hundred million starts to look careless.'

To escape politics, she skips to the subject of Leakzilla and its never-ending revelations. 'What's brutal is we're never outliving this,' she comments. 'Literally, it'll take decades to sift through it all. Years from now, people will still be losing jobs over this. It's like unexploded war munitions that go off a century later, you know? Oh, wow!' she says, tracking their arriving food. 'That looks *amazing*.'

They dig in, she groaning with pleasure at each mouthful, which stirs Tim's loins in a manner that, quite frankly, he deems inappropriate to a family-dining setting. He's barely able to taste, and orders himself not to gaze any lower than her chin.

'One thing Leakzilla did give us?' she says between

bites. 'Made me realize that privacy isn't just about people not peeping when I'm in the shower.'

His stomach does a loop-the-loop.

'Don't you think,' she goes on, 'privacy is actually, like, the right to be different in different situations? Know what I mean? Being different is *not* being fake. And if it is, then maybe fake is a good thing. Because people were nicer before, right? Like, maybe a bit of fake is what's required to be decent.'

Everything she says sounds so smart, and this stresses him – he needs a clever insight, yet goes blank. He keeps eating, forking it in faster, until his plate is clean, hers hardly touched. To save himself, he paraphrases something he heard on the radio: that ever since Leakzilla, you have this feeling you're being spied on. And, in a way, we *were* being spied on; just didn't know. All our private letters were kept by someone else, and monetized by some big-tech corp. 'Isn't that right?' He looks up, entirely uncertain. She's chewing, nodding. So he continues: 'And now? It's like someone could be listening to my thoughts all the time. Or does that make me sound like a whacko?'

'No, you're totally right. Know what's even more crazy? We are probably having the *exact* same conversation as everyone else in the whole world right now.'

Tim takes this as high endorsement. His hope rises. 'Hey, this is so great. I mean, hanging out.' Realizing how mawkish this is sounding, he adds, 'Well, so far.'

She looks at her handbag, which is ringing, then fishes out an iPhone, and sweeps aside her hair. 'Hey, you … Nah, can't talk … No, yeah. I will … No, I'm going to … I *will*, I swear. Stop buggin' me … Bye … Love you. Bye.' She hangs up, shakes her head, thumbs in a quick text message, sneaking a bite of crab's leg with the other hand. 'Sorry — my sister.'

'Everything good?'

She pauses, a naughty smile, then confesses. She and her sister always call when the other is on a date. If it's going terribly, you can just claim a family emergency, and get out of there.

'I feel flattered that I'm not a family emergency.'

She laughs. 'My sister's just nosey is the problem. Sorry — let me zing her this message. Okay, done. Where were we?'

'I was — you were saying everyone's having the same conversation?' His own smartphone, which is on vibrate, buzzes in his jeans. As she laments Leakzilla, he nods gravely, surreptitiously drawing his phone from his pocket to ensure that it's nothing urgently work-related. Keeping the phone out of sight under the table, he takes the stealthiest glance downward, then back at her.

What he saw was odd. The person who sent that message is sitting across from him. She must've zinged off that text, intending it for her sister, but had the messaging app open to her earlier chain with Tim, where she was apologizing for lateness. This latest text was short enough that he absorbed it in that furtive peek: 'Nice guy but not an A-lister, to be blunt.'

Tim sits there, hearing nothing, smile waxy. He thought they'd clicked. What did she want in a guy? Some creep with a pink Ferrari? In which case, why chat with me online in the first place? Despite bruised pride, or because of it, he finds her even more desirable. She turns down dessert, immune to the allure of a chocolate bag. When he tries to fill her glass, she places her hand over its mouth. 'Gotta work tomorrow.'

I have only a few minutes left, he recognizes. This is my last chance. Then I never see her again. But I *must* see her again. This isn't just another date. This is my life. I'm running out of time here. I haven't met anyone like this in so long. Then get to the point, man! Use your secret weapon. 'Hey, I know we both ticked the box for "liberal" in our profiles.'

'Yeah. I was wondering about that. Regarding you.'

'So, okay, I'll come clean.' He adopts a hush, leaning across the table. 'I don't publicize this around here. But if you ask me, Trump is the best thing for this country. Did we really want Hillary, sticking us with years more of Clinton corruption, ripping away our guns, and opening the borders wide as they could go?'

'You have guns?'

'No. But I should be able to get one, right? And I couldn't
have. I mean, if Hillary won it, I wouldn't. Anyway.' He
coughs nervously. 'Thing about progressives in this country
is they talk all this hopey-changey crap, right? But hope
and change is what *Trump* is all about. Right? And ever
since the election, it's these liberals whining about how bad
change is, how the sky is falling. What happened to hope
and change? Only if it's their side? Liberals are always
hating on their fellow Americans. Hating on Christians.
Hating on our democracy, saying they don't like the result,
so it must've been some lousy foreigners like the Russians.
Meantime, all that Trump voters wanted was someone who
won't bullshit. Yes, he's got his flaws. But who doesn't? I,
for one, am so tired of all the politically correct bull.' He
sniffs, offering a fast-fading grin. 'At least Trump will say
"Islamic" when saying "terrorism". And he cares about
jobs, not just transgender toilets. Normal people in this
country, we're sick of pointy-headed intellectuals telling us
how to live, right? Because *we* live in the real world. And

in the real world, "studies" and "statistics" don't matter. Still, I got to warn you about something: you can't say jack squat in this city. In Portland, you're not allowed to criticize anyone. Except if they're "white trash". Which is just as racist as words we're not supposed to say for black folks.'

'Uhm, you do know I'm African-American, right? You do see that.'

'Yeah, obviously! And, hey, I'm not saying those other words are okay. I am *not* a racist. Clearly. Or why'd we be out tonight?' He's crumbling, but compelled to keep going. As a last hope, he plays his trump card. 'You voted for him, too. I *know* you did.'

'Wait – what?' She cocks her head, eyes scrunched in puzzlement, opening slowly on him. '*I* voted for Donald Trump? Are you on crack right now?'

'Did you? Or didn't you?'

'You are definitely on crack. What makes you even *say* that?' Her phone is ringing again. Distractedly, she reaches into her bag, pushes her hair back. 'Hey, this is Boo … Yeah, I texted you already … I did, Kell … Something's wrong with your phone then … Uh-huh.' She drops the iPhone in her bag, and tells Tim: 'I actually need to get going.'

'Family emergency?' he says with a forced smile.

'No, no. Just need to get up early tomorrow.'

But he's still processing something. 'Why'd you answer, "This is Boo" to that person?'

'Because that's what I'm called.'

His stomach clenches. He looks at her. This isn't Nelly Haas. Maybe that was the name of the designer who replaced her. Those emails he read – they belonged to a completely different person. He spent hours spying on someone he'll never meet. *Such* an idiot. He can only stare down at the table.

The waiter deposits the check, and Tim hurriedly tries to pay. She reminds him about splitting it. 'We agreed to go American on this, remember?'

He slides his credit card beside hers.

'I'm being careful not to read your name off it,' she says.

'Tim Kalogerakis,' he tells her boldly, holding up the

credit card, as if standing naked before her. 'Nice to meet you. Nice to have met you.'

She fails to respond with her own name. 'Watch out there, Tim – I could go home and Zilla you. Just kidding.' What she means is: I'm obviously not looking *you* up.

Well, Tim tells himself, this is my punishment for violating an honor date. He glances around: at other diners wanting this night to last, at the hard-working waitstaff wanting this shift to end. None of us has any reason to care about politics. The billionaires get us fighting to protect *their* wallets. Not like we'll ever even see those guys in person! But me and this human being across the table – we liked each other. Then I run her off the road with bullshit that doesn't even concern us. What do *I* care about conservatives and liberals? I care about a few friends, too many of whom went cold these past years, maybe because of dumbass things I typed and hit 'send' on ages back. But was that me? Was it? I can't say what in hell I believe. Do my emails know better than I do?

He sees her out to Burnside, and she thanks him for

introducing her to Jake's. He is gracious, but worn down. This feels worse than a bad date; it's as if something important ended tonight. 'By the way, your sister was right. You didn't text her.' He takes out his phone, holds up the message from earlier, reading it aloud: 'Nice guy but not an A-lister, to be blunt.'

She turns her back to him, curls forward in shame. 'Fuck, fuck, fuck. I am totally mortified.'

'I'd ask if you had a good time, but ...' He shrugs, a little chuckle.

She's looking at him again, those shiny brown eyes, insisting the text was *not* how she thought of him, that she didn't ever talk of people as 'A-listers' — it was something stupid just to get rid of her sister.

He knows this isn't true, but lets her finish. 'So what *did* you think of me then?' he asks, dreading her reply. 'G'ahead. Tell me.'

'Damn! You are direct, Tim. I'm not saying it to your face.'

'See? Can't have been too good!'

She protests, saying she's merely embarrassed, and suggests an alternative: they'll message each other later with their honest impressions.

'No more texts,' he says. 'Please. I can't take any more of your texts.'

'Email. We'll go old-school. I'll be candid. And it won't be bad. I swear.'

Tim was expecting never to see her again. Any additional contact is better than he imagined, even if it means a hurtful review. So he agrees.

She stopped using her old email account after Leakzilla, setting up a fresh one with a complex mix of letters and numbers that are proving impossible to remember. She types it into his Contacts, and takes down his email address, too.

'What *I* see happening,' he tells her, 'is I'll be the only one of us to write.'

'No, no – I'm true to my word. What we'll do is this: we both write something, then, at exactly midnight tonight, we hit send. That way nobody gets to read the other's first and rewrite accordingly. It'll keep us honest. Sound fair?'

He offers to find her a taxi, but she already has an Uber coming.

Tim walks all the way home alone. Once safely inside, he hangs upside-down in his gravity boots, needing to shake out this ache. That thing about emailing at midnight wasn't for real – she needed to escape an awkward farewell. He's certainly not baring his heart by email ever again.

Hanging there, he ponders what he would have said. At five to midnight, he inverts, gets out of the boots, and awakens his phone, chest suddenly tight, like in high school before an exam that he'd told himself didn't matter – only to realize it *did*, and that it was too late.

I need to write something! I can't let this go. She was the smartest, most interesting, most attractive woman in *years*.

He opens his Contacts, which contains scores of names. The teenager at T-Mobile transferred his old list, and he has no recollection of who most of these people are. Except now she is somewhere in there. And he doesn't know her name.

Tim shuts his eyes, shakes his head. 'I am such an idiot.' He clicks aimlessly down the list, passing one unfamiliar person after another. If she emails him, he won't be able to respond until minutes later, which'll make it look like he cheated, waiting for her letter before having the guts for his own. He keeps scrolling, no hope left. Then he pauses upon reading a strange entry: 'Nelly Haas'. Wait, what?

That was the name of the person he looked up on Leakzilla. Maybe 'Boo' was just a nickname, what her sister calls her. Maybe those emails he read *were* hers. Maybe she wasn't hating him tonight. Maybe she was just looking for a way to gracefully admit her views, unsure how to confess to lying on an honor profile. Shit! I've got to write something *now*!

It's two minutes to midnight. If he was never great with language, he's even worse with touch screens. Madly, Tim pokes at the smartphone, carpenter's fingers wreaking havoc on autocorrect. He cannot find the words; he can't even find the letters.

In panic, he checks his inbox. Before his eyes, her email lands at exactly midnight. He almost opens it. But if his message reaches her even a little late, it'll be obvious he cheated. And he's *not* cheating this time. It did him no good before. He finishes his sentence, and hits send on a stumbling, typo-filled admission of how much he feels for her already, how she's the best person he's met in so long, how he *has* to see her again.

He opens her email, his leg jiggling. 'Hey Tim! Thanks again for tonight. Really cool to meet you. Okay, so I gotta start with an admission here. So, after we went our separate ways tonight, all I could think was what a cool guy you are.'

'Wahoo!' Tim runs back and forth across the room, eyes wide. Taking a breath, he reads on: 'You seemed so genuine to me, and that means a lot, especially when I'm just settling in this city. When I got home, I actually did something kind of naughty. I Zilla'd you. And I was blown away by what I found. I don't really care about liberal or conservative. But when you were talking tonight, you were so real. And I want that in a guy, someone who's super-genuine. But, Tim, you know what I found in your emails. And I can't date that guy. Tim, you voted Hillary.'

4

Sad! Wrong! Not Nice!

I WON'T CHANGE. BELIEVE ME. If you think I'm changing, you are wrong.

Before all this, I ran a hugely successful business, leasing aircraft to the best military juntas and the top rebels. I never broke a single law. Never. But anti-freedom bureaucrats had it in for me, and they rolled out the red tape, the US authorities bandying around vicious terms like 'Foreign Corrupt Practices Act'. It was harassment, pure and simple. Why not catch the bad guys for a change? Not an honest American whose only crime is wealth creation, a guy who's smart enough to organize his assets *around* the regulations, which is what you're supposed to do. The rules are highway dividers: you drive by them; only a moron runs directly into one. But I've got no delusions. A price *must* be paid. That is, paid by somebody else.

Oh, come on! You know I'm only trying to rile you. Forgive me if my humor's a little rusty. There's nobody else to talk to around here.

You should understand that, at the time of my death, a grand jury was prying most insensitively into a certain income of mine — an investigation far too dull to bore you with. Fortunately, reports emerged that I had plunged to my very timely demise in a plane crash deep in the Congolese jungle. The case halted, and I resumed — in Hanoi this time, with a name not necessarily corresponding to that assigned at birth, plus an array of well-stocked bank accounts. I'm informed that a touching memorial service took place in my hometown of Kalamazoo, engineered by my younger brother, Glen. The event was standing room only, with musical performance, dance, and plentiful tears, because people love me. A terrific event; really fantastic.

So everything was great – that is, until a pack of weasels started sniffing at old emails of mine posted online because of Leakzilla. These were not nice folks: scummy student lawyers in the nation's capital, led by a poisonous little Nancy Drew who twigged that, notwithstanding my tragic demise, I continued to dispatch the occasional email. There's no respect for privacy anymore; it's disturbing, really.

And what happened next – *that* was the real crime. My savings were frozen. Because government is the real thief. And banks, too. They talk about 'your account', then just cut you off when they please. You get stuck in some customer-service nightmare where everything's 'recorded for training purposes', meaning you can't use big-boy language without getting banned. Finally, you're talking with some outsourced dunce who keeps saying: 'So sorry, sir. That's what our records indicate.' Nobody's accountable these days. Such a shame.

After this unjust turn of events – my money ripped off, my location leaked – I was an innocent man on the run. Luckily, I'm highly resourceful. You won't find anyone more resourceful. So I contact my old friend Baz Grimaldi; great guy. We met during the good old days in Libya at the Corinthia Hotel – the only place to stay in Tripoli, next time you're in town. Grimaldi, like me, stands out of the pack. This guy exudes that Italian charm. Not only did he travel with a personal chef, but he brought along Italian waiters, too. A class act. And a born entrepreneur, like me. He did great in the ex-Yugoslavia, repurposing local military hardware, moving it to areas in more pressing need, like Africa and the Mideast. He also innovated in the transportation industry, assisting the needy in their efforts to reach the European job market by raft. He dabbled in the entertainment sector as well, circumventing the absurd restrictions on the import of tobacco and recreational pharmaceuticals. On top of all this, Grimaldi had an admirable passion for the arts. I once saw him accept payment in the form of an ancient Eritrean obelisk – now *that* is style. On another occasion, he gave me a glimpse of his art collection. Stunning. A Van Gogh still life of poppies. A Picasso harlequin head. A Matisse, a couple of Monets, a Gauguin.

And when I needed a hand, Grimaldi couldn't have been more generous, flying me first to Belgrade aboard his private Lear, then arranging to have me escorted via tinted-window Bentley down to the Adriatic coast of Albania by a chauffeur so smooth I could've rested a glass of milk on the dashboard. A speedboat zipped me across the water to Bari, then a motorbike deposited me at my present abode. Two months now, I've sojourned here in the glorious sunny south of Italy. And I'll be honest with you: I'm losing my fucking mind.

You see, this isn't Milan. Ain't Florence. Not even Naples or Palermo. I'm in Vizzacaro. Heard of it? Keep it that way. The heel of the boot stepped on this place and ground it into the earth. A village so small the locals dream of someday hitting it big in the next village along, which is itself about the smallest berg you ever saw.

Vizzacaro, shall I compare thee to a summer's day? Thou art more graffitied and more humid. The place is a few dozen new-build residences, each about to crumble, as if set up purely for insurance when the next earthquake strikes. Beyond the village limits is red earth, far as the eye can see. In Vizzacaro itself, the only green is weeds on what passes for Main Street, a lane where you could sit and read a whole magazine before even *hearing* a car engine. Not that you'd find a magazine worth leafing through. All we've got is a butcher, a grocery store, and a knick-knack shop vending chewing gum, crossword puzzles, and a bunch of indecipherable Italian newspapers.

At my house, there's not even internet, just an old TV with a smattering of local channels broadcasting psychics. The only English-language show is a British kids' program called *Andy's Baby Animals*. If the newly expanded staff at Guantanamo is listening right now, I encourage you to consider relaying broadcasts of *Andy's Baby Animals* to your more intractable prisoners. Waterboarding is nothing compared.

Grimaldi told me to keep a low profile around here, which is impossible. What you have is a meat-and-potatoes United States of American male in his mid-forties, sporting a Detroit Tigers baseball cap and cargo shorts, not speaking a word of their language. I don't exactly blend in. But were anyone to ask, I have a cover story – that is, I stole one from my little brother. Don't worry, I'm not saying I'm here doing secret work for Starbucks; I have my pride. My claim is that I'm a writer, holed up here putting together a sci-fi play, some idea that Glen once dribbled about, where this crusading young woman discovers an online portal that shows how everyone's about to die in some looming catastrophe. Typical bedwetter crap. But as it happens, I've had no opportunity to use his plot because the locals just wave me away, claiming not to know a word of English. At the very least, they're capable of discussing the finer points of *Andy's Baby Animals*. My guess is they're not allowed to talk with me.

So, I spend much of my time at the house, one of the few old buildings in town, a sprawling, five-bedroom white-stone complex with marble floors and a walled garden at the back with a lemon grove and stray cats everywhere, the mangiest you can picture. I feed them sometimes. I'm telling you: I'm a good guy. Other times, I throw water at them, which is pretty funny. And it gets hot down here, so it's nice of me, too.

As Grimaldi promised, everything is taken care of in Vizzacaro. If I encounter the slightest problem, I'm to go directly to the mayor, who lives next door. I have no cash myself but food arrives daily, three meals placed on my doorstep by the mayor's maid, Shani, the only village resident more conspicuous than I am: a bosomy, wide-hipped, middle-aged African woman who can't see. What matters to me is that she's a solid cook. As for the mayor, he's a dimple-cheeked old fogey, always stroking his thick white mustache, never without a smile – past eighty, I'd guess, but still running his medical practice, in addition to leading the annual Sagra del Carciofo fair, a pagan holdover where the locals worship artichokes. I'm fucking serious right now. On my arrival, the mayor came over with a bottle of grappa, and talked until he ran out of English words, which didn't take long, after which we sat in my garden, gazing up at stars, these high walls surrounding us. To look at the darkness overhead, as I have every night since that first, is to realize that I'm in an open-air jail.

To fill my time until I figure a way out of here, I've sunk low: books. Besides a couple of hundred tomes in Italian, the house contains a handful of English-language volumes, all romances by Nicholas Sparks. Masochistically, I've read every one – *Message in a Bottle*, *The Notebook*, *Nights in Rodanthe*, *A Walk to Remember*, *Dear John*, *Safe Haven* – telling myself there's a use in wading through this drivel, that I might tweeze out the human weaknesses that these stories work on. And I found something. All of these books, after hundreds of pages of tripe, end with the same conclusion: people change.

Why, I ask myself, do folks need to believe that life will transform you? Why *that* message, over and over? I guess they want to be convinced that living – which has no point, is dismal for most of them, then stops dead – at least made them wiser. That's right, guys: embrace your lousy lives! It's all for the best!

This said, who sits around reading made-up stories anymore? A person needs to be stranded, with no other options. In the future, mark my words, literature will be exclusively for the incarcerated.

After I completed my Nicholas Sparks marathon, I turned to the only coffee-table book, *Vicious People Doing Stupid Things*, a selection of snapshots by the celebrity photographer Georgina Peet. The foreword, by Gore Vidal, describes this trashy junk as 'high art', which gets me thinking about Grimaldi's collection. He can't sell those paintings on the open market, given that they're – according to so-called experts – classed as 'stolen works that remain unrecovered'. It's a tragedy, really. Because this kind of restrictive definition only punishes the public, who'd love nothing more than to line up like ants to stare at pictures of fruit bowls.

But Grimaldi is no fool. Accumulating those works was an act of genius. As he explained, his attorney can always dangle the prospect of rescuing a long-lost artwork before any meddling prosecutor. 'Retract these slanders against my client, and he may reciprocate with a good-faith act of his own, moving heaven and earth to recover a Matisse long believed burned by Romanian thieves – but perhaps *not* burned. Perhaps in a warehouse somewhere. Does the government prefer to proceed with childish allegations against Mr. Grimaldi – charges that are sure to be refuted in court? Or would you, Mr. Prosecutor, care to *personally* restore a priceless artwork to civilization? Your call.' Only a barbarian would refuse.

I smirk – it occurs to me why I'm down here. I myself am another priceless masterpiece, stashed out of sight, kept from prying eyes, awaiting the time when Grimaldi might require a bargaining chip to hand the pesky authorities. After all, the penal systems of several reputable nations are eager to take charge of my housing for the next fifteen to thirty years. While it's flattering to realize you are akin to a great work of art, that is not the role I aspired to. Yet the first step for a rat to escape his cage is to realize he's *in* a cage. Only, I lack any way to gnaw my way out of here.

So I approach my sole contact in Vizzacaro, the mayor, and press him to arrange a talk with Grimaldi, from whom I've not heard a word since my arrival.

Two weeks pass. Nothing happens. So I ask again. Once more, the mayor merrily agrees. And nothing happens. He has, I realize, a well-honed tactic. If asked, he *always* agrees. And doesn't move a finger. The applicant gathers cobwebs, and finally gives up. Only, I don't give up.

But I did tell a small lie. To dramatize my awful reading choices, I stated that there were no books in English other than those romance novels. But there is one, and I'd consider it a practical joke, if Grimaldi had wit. It's a copy of *Purgatorio*, the second part of Dante's *Divine Comedy*, in a dual-text edition, Italian on the left-hand page, English translation on the right. Nicholas Sparks, you got nothing on this, because *Purgatorio* is the ultimate redemption story. Nothing hastens transformation like a poker darted in your backside by a highly motivated demon.

Pondering this pretty image, I can't help but admire the sales executives who came up with the notion of purgatory – such a fine way to control the sheeple. The idea, if I have it right, is that God made everyone and He knows everything – yet it's humans who have control, so they should be punished for wrongdoing. How do believers square all that? They don't even try. People are just algorithms, doing as they're told. It's funny when you consider how humanity passed through all those centuries of civilizing, moving beyond their beastly origins, first creating god-worship, then scientific enlightenment, finally adding those cute fantasies about 'human rights' – only to return back where they started, living above all for animal appetites: curating their food, their sex, their babies. Even the lowest creatures didn't fritter away the last millennia on crackpot notions – they knew all along that life is just chomping and fucking. There's transformation for you!

All this talk about appetites is making me hungry, so I go to the back door to collect my lunch. I find a bare step. The blind African maid is forcing me to nibble leftovers from the fridge. Not nice! Irritated, I stride across the lane to the mayor's house, and hear voices from inside. I open his front door and find a somber scene within: most of the villagers around a daybed, where the mayor lies, his mortal soul having departed for parts unknown, perhaps now learning that purgatory, alas, already has a mayor. As I re-enter my own house, I wonder what my angle should be. Grimaldi's employees will learn of this sooner or later. Another arrangement might await me. Or have I just become a little more complicated?

More pressing than the mayor's inconsiderate passing is my hunger. Nobody has yet provided lunch. It's inhumane: this maid just halts meal service the instant her employer croaks? I frown into the open fridge, ignoring that cat outside, which keeps scratching to get in. No scraps for you today. Could I eat a cat? It'd be frowned on. And not that meaty. So I pour myself a glass of water to throw at the pest. I open the door to the garden, but it must've scampered off. Yet that scratching persists. It's coming from the outside cellar. I go out there. Through its frosted-glass door, I detect the form of a large mammal. I return to the house, fetch a tennis racket and a butcher's knife.

When I fling open the cellar door, it's Shani. She raises her hands and makes a shushing noise. I don't like to be shushed, so ask, 'What happened with my lunch?'

'The door,' she says, meaning to the cellar, 'it closed on me. I cannot get out.' I never knew she spoke English. This could come in handy. But first, I turn detective.

'You poisoned his spaghetti or strangled him or something?'

'Sorry?'

'Did you kill the mayor?'

'If I kill that man, I kill him many years ago. No, no.' Owing to her blindness, Shani doesn't mind that the cellar light is out, but I can barely see down here. So I invite her up into the house, sit her down, and pose questions. She has lived in Vizzacaro, it turns out, for eighteen years, ever since an accident blinded her.

'How did the mayor come to hire you?'

'Hire me? He keeps me here.'

The terms of her employment are not what you'd call voluntary. Nor was she chained up; I saw her loping across the lane often. Can't have been *that* bad. But, Shani explains, the sweet, dimpled, white-mustachioed mayor confiscated her documents way back, and refused to allow her money to go anywhere. In the early days, he provided other strong reasons to stay, she adds darkly, which I take to mean that he beat her if she dared venture off. Not that she could've gone far without working eyes or cash.

'Everybody in Vizzacaro, they know I am here. Nobody helps me. Nobody does anything.'

I smile because we're in the same boat: both imprisoned in this dump! I almost point out that now is her chance, that she should run back home, wherever that might be. But I stop myself. 'You must be starving,' I say, because I am, and cannot allow an artiste of the saucepan to quit town without creating a few more choice dishes. Shani is afraid to go buy food, since everyone will be wondering what became of her. 'Well, we're in a bind because I haven't got a cent,' I tell her. She reaches into her bra, and draws out a wad of cash that she took off the dead man.

I return with all the groceries that she requested, and Shani works wonders, first familiarizing herself with the kitchen set-up at my place, expertly using touch, smell and taste to navigate the stove top. I keep all the windows shuttered lest anyone sees that she has migrated across the lane. When my food is ready – huge, fatty meatballs, as I requested – she stands by the table while I eat, trying to ingratiate herself, believing I hold some sort of power.

Maybe I do.

The next day, I advise her to leave town. She has a bit of money. And her tormentor is laid out in a funeral parlor by now. Get a train to Rome – there'll be a Kenyan immigrant population to help her there. And we'll keep in touch, I say – this last part because I want to know how it's done. Will anyone stop us wandering away now that the mayor is turning to dust?

But Shani won't risk it. How could she even get to the closest train station? She could perhaps sneak out of the village by night without anyone noticing. But then? We're miles from anywhere. Obviously, she can't drive. She needs an accomplice.

During the following days, she takes up residence in one of my extra rooms, mostly quiet in there, only the soft sweep of her hand running across the walls, or the mumble of her prayers. My fine dining continues apace and, bit by bit, she recounts her years with the mayor.

Shani arrived in Italy during the Nineties from a Nairobi slum. A local tough guy there had promised her work as a housecleaner in Italy, she tells me, though I suspect she knew her real work would be men. And so it was, until one day she was bashed by a client and dumped on a roadside near Bari, the Adriatic on one side, an empty motorway on the other. In fear of capture by the police, she hid, unable to flag another client in a zone where prostitutes never operated – not to mention her torn clothes and banged-up face. Few vehicles passed, most speeding by. Then an eggshell-blue sports car drifted toward her, trundling down the grassy shoulder. She stood, and waved, seeing that the driver was a woman. Then Shani realized: both the driver and passenger were asleep. She tried to get away, her scream awakening the driver, who made eye contact with Shani. The car clipped her, flinging her in the air. She awoke, twisted and smashed, gazing at what was the sky. But day had gone dark. Voices approached. An Englishwoman speaking to a man about how she couldn't have avoided the lady, and what was she even *doing* in the road – that, Jesus, she looks half dead, what the fuck do we do? Shani was too badly wounded to utter a word, let alone move. The couple stood above her, the man pressing something crunchy into Shani's hand. Their car engine started, and drove away. Shani clasped her fingers; it was currency.

When she woke again, it was still dark, but freezing now, the wind whipping over the waves. She wobbled to her feet, then fell, her right leg excruciating, unable to sustain her. She sat there, breathless from pain, rubbing her eyes, which refused to work. 'The first car that stops for me, it is Mr. Mayor. He drives me to his house. He helps me to get better.'

'Yes, right – he was a doctor. And what about your eyes?'

'Those cannot come back. The problem is in my head.'

'Damage to your brain?'

'Yes, yes. So Mr. Mayor, he is lonely. When I can, I help him as thanks. I try to cook for him, too. This is hard when I cannot see. But he wants it, so I learn all the Italy dishes. He tells me how Italian people, how they like their food, and I can do that. Then I am mostly better, and I start talking about, "I am go away now" and "I find hospital to help my eyes." Mr. Mayor, he tells me how much more nice is here in Vizzacaro. Is safe also, nobody hurting me. No men, like the one that beats me and leaves. One night, I am thinking, "Okay, maybe I like to go away." I try to find my documents. I cannot find them.'

'Maybe you lost them in the accident.'

'No, I have them when I come with Mr. Mayor. Also, my money is gone, too.'

'All right, but *eighteen years*? You never seriously tried to leave? Doesn't show much initiative, Shani!'

She shakes her head, not understanding.

'You didn't try to leave *ever*? Or tell anyone?'

'Each time, something strange. Like, I am walking toward the big road, and a car bumps into me again – just little bump. Not so bad as before, but like warning, you know? And I say, "Who is there?" And it's no sound.'

'Nobody in the village helped you?'

'Helped? They are the ones hitting me with a car. Anything I do, they are telling him.'

As you can imagine, my mind was drifting during this sob story. So I fetch the Italian newspaper that I bought earlier, and get her to translate. To do this, I must read the words phonetically, and she deciphers bits here and there. I need to learn what's happening stateside, especially if it has a bearing on me. And, I confess, I take pleasure updating myself on the winding-down of the American Empire. Every empire falls, of course, but I never expected this one to crumble so entertainingly and in such a hurry. One minute, it's Yankee do-gooders haranguing the world about democracy; next minute, they're all whimpering about their own elections, just because the votes didn't come out like they wanted. We never *really* liked democracy. We just like our guys to be the winner. You hear people say how disastrous Obama was, but I celebrate that guy. Because the legacy of every president is who succeeds him. And I thank you, Obama, for who came next.

To be clear, I never much cared for democracy myself. Look around: do you *honestly* want those people to have a vote that counts exactly as much as yours? That said, democracy did work in America this last presidential election. Had I been there, I'd have voted for Trump at least once. Because his message was right: we are *the* most talented, *the* most generous, *the* kindest, smartest, most caring, honest, warm-hearted people in history. We're also the best at sports. Everything good is either *in* America, or *by* America. Shit, we invented sitting in Starbucks, getting pissy about the Wi-Fi! 'Excuse me, this connection is crap. I totally can't read my Facebook newsfeed. And I asked for double whip on my iced caramel frap. I am *not* paying for this.'

Oh, America – like my barista brother – you've grown into the most adorable dud. Begging to be dominated. But by whom? As a businessman, I look globally for opportunity. See a failing corporation, then you must ask, Who can fill that gap in the market? A popular choice for the post-America victor is China, but I can't see it myself. And who says the next empire has to be a country? Could be hackers. Or a few well-chosen strongmen. Or a handful of top companies – the very best, most beautiful corporations. If *I* had to bet? I'd say the future belongs to our phones. Their offspring will grow up to rule the world. And what fantastic news. Because, when the old rules dissolve, a new and better order takes control: power. Strange as it'll seem to future generations, there was a depressing time not long ago when weaklings had all sorts of control. But the future is looking bright. I see that. And I'm a smart guy. I make terrific predictions. Believe me.

'I do not know if they can recognize me today,' Shani is saying, though I have no idea why.

'What and who?' I ask.

She's been speaking, it turns out, of her husband and two sons in Kenya. The boys will have grown up, and her spouse has surely remarried.

'Well,' I tell her, 'keep cooking delicious meals like that, and I'll do what I can to help you.'

'That's what the mayor always said.'

As the week goes on, a strange atmosphere develops between us. More than two months had passed without me really speaking to anyone, so I've been aching to talk. But I'm also in overload at the stimulation, and get rattled when Shani chatters, so must cut her off. One night, she tried to seduce me – not with much seriousness, but perhaps because she feared not doing so. I considered going along with her, but I'm not attracted, so I told her there's no need, that she's safe here, which is true.

I've gotten in the habit of doing our grocery shopping each morning, using that money she pickpocketed from the mayor. I also buy an Italian newspaper, and have Shani translate. At night, we watch TV, she interpreting the wisdom of the sexy showgirls on the sidelines of almost every Italian show.

Over these days, I must confess, Shani and I establish a weird connection, both of us trapped here, sharing meals, sharing conversation, each wondering how this ends. I tell her it's a matter of time. Grimaldi – when I say the name, she looks scared – he'll send someone for me sooner or later. She asks if I'll be talking to the man himself, and begs me that, if he asks, I assure him she never saw *anything* bad here.

Which tells me how much she must've seen. The mayor protected her, keeping her as his concubine. Now, she has no guardian, so needs desperately for me to become her new angel. And I have a heart; I am human. I also see something very clearly: she needs to leave before Grimaldi learns that she's here. Shani won't be high on his to-do list, but she must not be hanging around when his people arrive. After dinner, I again counsel her to go. She's so afraid to travel alone. Can't I help her?

Perhaps. I ponder how we get out of this.

The next afternoon, a couple of young guys pull up

in a dirty Alfa Romeo outside the mayor's old house, and start honking the horn, who knows why. They're street rats around twenty years old, wearing Carrera shades, minimum-wage spiked hair, neck tattoos, torn designer jeans. A village elder, deferential, head down, hobbles out to speak with them.

I hold still at the shutter slats inside my house, peeking out. Shani is cooking a porcini risotto to go with my steak. I whisper for her to come over *right now* and translate what they're saying. She hears only a snippet before they enter the mayor's house – but it's enough for her to grasp my hand. She has heard those voices before. They are boys from Bari. Nearly stumbling in her haste, she feels her way across the kitchen wall, knocking a saucepan off the stove, then finds the stairs into the back garden, sliding the heels of her bare feet down each riser, gauging the height of the step, legs trembling. Once outside, she's penned in by high garden walls, terrified, and marching unsteadily toward the cellar. 'Hide me. Please, please.'

I can hardly say no to Shani. We've grown close

these past days. She shuts herself in, goes still, silent in the dark.

They are banging at my front door. I make my way there, slipping on my shoes as I go. Their employer, they inform me in broken English, is waiting for me. They lead me to their car, sit me in the front passenger seat. We burn out of the village, windows down, breeze flicking at my hair. The landscape rushes by: gnarled olive trees in dry red earth. I haven't seen this terrain since I arrived in Vizzacaro, and that was at night on a motorcycle. I recall certain movies, in which men are transported to meetings by gentlemen of Italian extraction, only to get a high-caliber bullet in the neck during the drive. But I refuse to indulge in stereotypes simply because this is southern Italy. Basile Grimaldi is an entrepreneur who appreciates wealth creation, just as I do. And he's a personal friend. Furthermore, who'd be so stupid as to shoot someone in their own car?

Miles pass before I remember that I neglected something important. The cats. I forgot to leave even a bowl of milk.

Even with pounding dance music on the car stereo, I hear in my mind the cats scratching on the door outside. Which reminds me of the day when the scratching was Shani in the cellar. She's down there now. And the door can't be opened from inside. She's trapped if I don't act. Nobody in that village would dare enter an empty house that belongs to Grimaldi. She'll die of thirst, discovered mummified months from now. I can't leave it like this.

Nor can I easily go back. If they knew I'd been speaking with her, they might assume I know whatever she does.

As the next mile passes, I can't stop thinking about her, locked in, scratching. Finally, I shout over the music: 'Guys!'

The driver glances at me, raises his chin, confused, still going ninety miles an hour.

'Hey, I left something. I need to go back.' I turn down the music, and repeat myself, more forcefully.

The guy in the back reaches his arm toward me, tapping the face of a giant wristwatch. 'Not possible,' he says. 'Not possible.'

'Yes, possible. Yes, possible.' To show I mean business,

I fling open my door, even though we're bulleting down the highway.

'Ohhhhhhhhh!' they shout in unison, the driver reaching across me to pull the door shut. '*Ma che CAZZO fai, cretino?*' he says, meaning who knows what, though nothing flattering.

'Go back there. Now.'

'We *no* go back!'

'We *yes* go back!'

He curses. But I repeat my order. And again.

Finally, the two confer. After much bitter griping, the driver takes an off ramp, guns it around, and roars us back toward the very village I've spent months yearning to escape. All the way, the driver is shouting at me in Italian.

We screech to a halt outside the house. The guys aren't interested in what I need, so they smoke in the car. I walk casually to the front door, then through the house, into the garden, to the cellar door. I press my ear to it. I hear Shani breathing in there.

I must pause matters here.

It drives me crazy that you think I've changed. That I've been transformed. Okay, maybe I was. Maybe it was reading about purgatory. Because you get out of purgatory. And so must she.

I place my hand on the doorknob. She says my name very softly, voice quavering. She has spent years in this village, and she's about to be set free. Before opening the door, though, I whisper to her: 'Stay *completely* quiet. Okay? Quiet. I'll be back.'

I return to the car, and look to the one in the back seat, who seems more serious. 'Something for your boss,' I say.

Back at the cellar door, the two guys flank me. I whisper for Shani, who stands there in the darkness, looking blindly past me.

'You're going,' I whisper to her. 'You get to leave.'

5

How the End Begins

S HE DOESN'T KNOW HIS full name, so the search takes time.

When Kelly first met the boy, he was begging outside her law school, emaciated, with hollow cheeks, a wispy goatee. Héctor's soft request, repeated to every passer-by: 'Give only what you can. Only what you can.' A filthy cardboard sign rested on his knees, stating that he'd served in Afghanistan, and this won Kelly's sympathy, she being a military brat, born in Okinawa, raised on a base in Germany, then Camp Lejeune, North Carolina, on to San

Diego, and finally Tampa. 'It wasn't the war that did this to me,' Héctor said of his scabby, inebriated condition. 'I ain't blaming nobody but me being a stupid sonofabitch.' A little smile followed, making him a kid again.

During her first two years attending G. W. Law, Kelly was always gathering small change, ensuring she had something to drop in his cup. Sometimes, she'd find him wasted, sprawled on the sidewalk, and he'd curse her out. Later, if he was needy again, he reverted to sweet and boyish. When she tired of this manipulation, Kelly snubbed him, refusing to hand out the quarters clinking in her backpack. Until he called her over, asking forgiveness for his rude tone, and she felt lousy – though never bad enough to apologize herself. Instead, she frostily placed a few dollars in his cup, awaiting the gratitude that she batted away. On those mornings when she found Héctor unconscious and too wrecked even to snarl, she knelt before him, pulling apart her blueberry muffin and feeding his gentle three-legged pitbull, Kimmo, until the dog disappeared for good. In much the same way, Héctor himself went. Perhaps arrested. Or cleaned up, and back home in Austin. His absence from the pavement was like a death without consequence, another human removed from the rolls.

When she saw other homeless people in the area, she asked after that Hispanic boy, the ex-soldier who begged around here. Most of the panhandlers in DC were too lost in their own psychoses to answer. But an obese black man with matted gray hair, his trousers held up by rope, said the ambulance took that guy. When Kelly was buying dinner at Whole Foods, she noticed a team of paramedics picking out snacks, and she inquired how one might track down a family member who'd ended up on the streets, then in the back of an ambulance. Kelly – who believed that she never told a lie – had unthinkingly claimed Héctor as a relative. But it was almost true. He was probably alone in some hospital ward, nobody looking out for him, another forgotten veteran – that made him family to her. She decided: I'm finding this guy.

So it is that Kelly finds herself lingering around an emergency department, pestering nurses and administrators.

Finally, she lands at the hospital's finance department, across from a fake-gruff native Hawaiian, who locates the bills of a twenty-nine-year-old indigent who might fit her description. The patient was just transferred out of ICU to a location that the Hawaiian lets her glimpse on his computer screen. 'You didn't get this from me,' he tells her. 'And if you see Mr. Melendez, please tell him we're still lacking payment details.'

Waiting for the elevator up, Kelly takes a squirt of antibacterial soap from the wall dispenser, pleased with herself at having cracked this case in a single morning. No great surprise for one whose family tree is packed with Texas lawmen! Her half-smile is because she's not genetically related to any of those folk, having been adopted with her sister (they, brown-skinned; the Haas family, white Texans who renamed the adorable twins Kelly and Nelly). Bloodlines aside, she does share her adoptive family's devotion to its military roots, which trace back for generations. Not just Texas Rangers, but confederate soldiers during the Civil War, infantry in WWII, officers in Korea and Vietnam, all the way up to Dad, a marine in both Iraq wars before retiring as lieutenant colonel.

Kelly herself expected to enlist, an intention formed on a Tuesday morning, September 11, 2001, when she was in fourth grade in North Carolina. Years later, at her Tampa high school, she always talked about joining military intelligence, only to be excluded after graduation because of a congenital hole in her heart, which medics guessed had resulted from her biological mother's substance abuse. Rage coursed through Kelly on the day of the rejection – that her fate should be determined by a stranger's mistakes. She believed in justice, that her country and her military embodied the principle. Yet this outcome was patently *un*just. After all, doctors had fixed her heart in an operation in Germany when she was one. It had never hampered her – she played volleyball through school, she jogged, you name it. People said she shouldn't have admitted anything on the form, that they'd never have known. But she was honest, so that was that.

The Haas family didn't tolerate wallowing, so she

picked herself up and enrolled at Florida State, majoring in modern history, a keen interest of hers since 9/11. After college, she waited tables, took junior marketing positions, did secretarial work, often toiling seventy hours a week. Even though it took years, Kelly was going to pay back every penny of student loans before law school, just as she'd planned on passing the bar before marriage, and marriage before kids, and so on until contented old age. Her future husband was himself already decided, Bryan R. Michelmore, loyal boyfriend since age sixteen, when a math teacher in Tampa told his class to solve a problem on the board: 'Partner up, you guys!' She and Bryan took the order to heart, and hadn't dissolved the partnership since. Everyone – even their parents way back – said they'd marry someday. She feels blessed for this, especially because her twin, Nelly – known as Boo in the family – is condemned to seeking love online since moving to work for Nike in Portland, landing dud after dud, among them a stalker met on HonrDate who refuses to stop bugging her with emails.

A nurse yanks the curtain aside, revealing Héctor propped up in bed, tidier and cleaner than Kelly has ever seen him, his gaze clear but his gut swollen like a beach ball, a needle protruding and plastic bag dangling, filling gradually with yellow liquid. As gallons of fluid are removed, his stomach gradually flattens. 'I'm so disgusting, man,' he says, teeth chattering. 'But I don't *feel* bad. That's weird, right?'

Although he's around her age, he still seems like a child – even more now that he's sober. Only the home-made tattoos on his hands and throat evoke the street. Oddly, he doesn't seem surprised to see her. Anyone would've sufficed – he just needs a person. Needs to speak. Needs to understand his situation, so talks compulsively. 'Something in my stomach got bursted, right? And I was, like, vomiting all this blood. It was crazy, man.' Coming off alcohol suddenly, you can die, so they kept a close eye on him. But Héctor insists he's doing great now.

Kelly has sympathy for addicts – with a thin lining of contempt. She never took a drink, a cigarette, a toke. The appeal escapes her. 'I'm just pleased to see you in one piece, Héctor.'

'But I'm so disgusting, right? Hey, where's that nurse? She needs to get this bag offa me, man.'

'She'll be back. I'm sure there're lots of other patients that need something.' This sounded scolding, so she brightens it. 'And you're doing pretty good, right? Focus on that.'

He agrees, but seems shifty, talking about how 'this special doctor I got' is coming soon, and could Kelly please stay, and ask some questions. She checks the time. Loads of homework today, so can't hang around *too* long. But he has nobody, and served our nation, which is more than Kelly can say of herself. 'But I do have to go by noon. Or, let's say, one at the latest. Would that work?'

'Do only what you can,' he says, head bowed.

To assuage the guilt, she takes his hand, shaking it, giving her name.

'I know who you are!' he lies. 'I remember. The girl from the college.'

'That's me.'

As they await the liver specialist, Kelly engages him in conversation, but he's capable of only one subject: that he doesn't *feel* ill, as if pleading with her to confirm that it's nothing serious.

She reminds him that, as a veteran, he should have access to Walter Reed Medical Center, just down the road from here. He becomes evasive at this, and it dawns on her: this guy wasn't ever on active duty; that was just for donations. For an instant, she's indignant. But look at him. How angry can she be? And, after all, he's a fellow American. Not for me to judge.

The liver specialist sweeps in without identifying herself, hastily summarizing the nature of the illness as if lecturing pre-meds about advanced cirrhosis. Héctor keeps saying he's not touched a drink since they brought him in. 'They don't even let me, man! Even if I wanted!' When asked about his alcohol abuse, he recounts a history of horrors: violent parents who introduced him to drugs and booze in early childhood; getting drunk daily from age eight; sniffing solvents and glue. This shocks Kelly, who never even had the chance to decline a sip of booze until age fourteen at a party. The doctor merely nods at Héctor's account, a gaze of detachment, as if she wants to get back to *her* facts: how his Gamma-GT levels are too high, how his spleen is dangerously swollen, and the pancreas, too. Liver transplants require a patient to be dry for at least six months, and then you're just on a waiting list. Plus, transplants for substance abusers are always controversial, she warns. 'But you *are* young, so that could work in your favor. Still, there are tough facts to face.'

'Six months clean? I can do that.'

'In your experience, Doctor,' Kelly asks, 'what's ahead for Héctor in this period when he stays dry?'

The doctor nods to acknowledge the question, avoiding eye contact, reaching for Héctor's shoulder to address him directly. 'Have we spoken about timescales yet? Has anyone had that conversation with you?' She lays out the meaning of MELD scores, and where he is on that range. 'You're at forty. Statistically – by which I mean looking at very large numbers of people,' the doctor explains, tensing up. 'Statistically, we would probably be expecting a 71 per cent mortality in three months. But those are statistics only.'

Héctor looks blankly at the specialist. When she falls silent, he gives a tight little chuckle. Kelly asks if the doctor might kindly drop back later, once he's had the chance to absorb all this. The doctor concurs, the curtain swishes aside, and it's just Kelly and Héctor again. Eyes blank, he repeats how he doesn't believe in numbers. 'I ain't dying in, like, three months! Look at me, man! What did she say, like, thirty per cent don't have mortality?'

Kelly is glad to have been a sympathetic face at this awful moment, but she cannot become the support worker to a stranger. She has her own duties: law school, her family, Bryan. She cannot allow all of that to suffer out of an act of kindness. She expresses hope that he liked seeing her again, the implication being that this is her only visit.

'Bye,' he says, barely looking her way.

Back home, she closes the apartment door behind herself, eyes shutting fast; she takes a long, deep breath.

Resume normal life. She'd like to phone Boo, but can't face recounting this morning. And she has tons of work. She orders herself to get at it.

Off the bed, she grabs her silver MacBook, and sets herself up on a stool at the breakfast bar – the closest that she and Bryan get to a dining area in their tiny one-bedroom. The building is pre-war art deco, south of Logan Circle, a six-minute jog to the White House, their neighbors mostly gay and lesbian couples with dogs (little dogs for the gay dudes, big dogs for the lesbians). Other residents include government contractors who need a crash pad in the capital, and out-of-state political operatives who visit DC as rarely as possible. She and Bryan themselves won't stick around here forever. When they start a family, it'll be Virginia or beyond, depending on which law firm hires her. If he had his way, Bryan would move to the suburbs tomorrow and have kids the day after. But Kelly is holding off – they operate according to her schedule, and he accepts that.

Yet lately, something has shifted. She's developed an urge that almost embarrasses her, taking longing looks at others' children, wondering what age they are, what stage that is, suppressing a pang as she walks away. If one must choose between career and family, she'll take both. And in this muddled spirit, they've stopped using contraception recently. After sex, they fall silent, folded together, neither daring to name this new stage.

Kelly doesn't have time to dwell on it – too much work. She drags over a pile of textbooks for the digital-law clinic. Last year, she scored a coup regarding a shady Michigan businessman, Fleming Pilczuk, who was reported dead in Africa a couple of years back. Kelly was part of a team poring over reams of documents revealed by Leakzilla, and discovered that an email address associated with the Pilczuk account continued to send messages long after his supposed death, including asking his mother in Kalamazoo to arrange a memorial in his honor. Kelly's discovery became national news, restarted a grand-jury investigation, and culminated in Pilczuk's arrest in Italy, where he was handed to the authorities by the respected Italian entrepreneur and politician Basile Grimaldi. The Pilczuk case then took a curious turn, becoming a conservative cause trumpeted by Sean Hannity of Fox News, who has been railing nightly against the outrage of a foreign detention of this US businessman. As Hannity explains to his audience, Europe today is nothing but a bunch of multicultural feminazis, overrun with sharia law – thankfully, elements that will never cross the Atlantic during the current administration. Under sustained pressure from Hannity, the United States government has no choice but to act, and is currently negotiating Pilczuk's release into American custody, where he can enjoy fair and balanced justice. The case has brought Kelly considerable attention at law school, making her something of a star in her year. Now she must maintain this momentum to get hired by a top firm.

Blowing at her steaming mug of coffee, she surfs the web for a few minutes, still troubled by this morning. She figured a person had to drink for decades to die from it. There *must* be a way back for Héctor. She types 'define' into Google, intending to add 'cirrhosis'. However, the search engine is impatient, popping up four guesses:

define **love**
define **pansexual**
define **sociopath**
define **narcissist**

She wonders why these predictions in particular appeared. Must've been an algorithm that parses all the searches in her region, then surmises what's on the mind of this latest typing human. She deletes 'define', and inputs 'why do', getting:

why do **we yawn**
why do **dogs eat grass**
why do **we cry**
why do **men have nipples**

She laughs at that last offering. Yeah, why *do* guys have nipples? Google is weird. People are weird. She types 'google is', and reads:

> google is **it going to rain today**
> google is **it going to rain tomorrow**
> google is **your friend**
> google is **gay**

She tries 'the internet is'. The answers, read in a row, come out like bad poetry:

> the internet is **not the answer**
> the internet is **a playground**
> the internet is **beautiful**
> the internet is **made of cats**

She tries 'human beings are', and gets:

> human beings are **a disease**
> human beings are **social animals**
> human beings are **members of a whole**
> human beings are **evil**

She puts in 'i think i':

> i think i **love you**
> i think i **have anxiety**
> i think i **have cancer**
> i think i **have adhd**

Then 'is anyone doing':

> is anyone doing **the housework**
> is anyone doing **anything about isis**
> is anyone doing **early tax loans**
> is anyone doing **anything about global warming**

Finally:

> it's time to
> it's time to **stop**
> it's time to **party**
> it's time to **say goodbye**
> it's time to **die**

Héctor didn't seem about to die. How could he go from today to nothing? She types in 'how do u die?' and hits enter. The search results include a life-expectancy calculator, an article on the dying process, and a 'Fun and Humorous Death Quiz'. Way down the list of results is a link to a site called 'How You Die'. She clicks on this, landing on what looks like a page designed circa 1999: pixelated purple text on a black background, the title flashing pointlessly.

A search box says, 'Name', the idea being to identify yourself, and read how the Grim Reaper will get you. It's a hoax site, probably to infect your computer. Yet she's tempted – to see what happens, as when standing before a carnival game that you know is fixed. So, she tests it out with celebrity names. The site seems to output random diseases, usually a cancer or a stroke or pneumonia. What kind of person produces such a webpage? The internet, she thinks, makes it so hard to respect humanity.

And yet Kelly can't stop herself typing in more celebrities she admires: President Trump and Kanye West and

Sweet J Vincent. There's something creepily addictive about this, fantasizing that the answers are right, and that she alone knows this. She finds herself typing in Héctor's name, too, but hesitates halfway. The site is entirely fake – so why does this feel wrong? As if, inputing his name, she might cause his demise. Which is absurd superstition. She won't let that rule her, so hits enter.

The answer stops her short. She leans back, trying to figure this out. It's a one-word response: 'Cirrhosis'. Okay, that's strange. How would it know that? It was probably just a random answer, so she types in Héctor's full name again, awaiting a different response. But again: 'Cirrhosis'.

She closes her browser, restarts the laptop, and walks across the room to the window over Mass Avenue, wanting to rouse herself, and return to the real world. Yet she immediately comes back and types his name again, demanding that the algorithm provide a different answer. But, no: it's the same. She's annoyed with herself now. The person who designed this webpage is having an effect, disturbing her, and that's what trolls want.

Does this site somehow have access to medical information? Is it some sort of disgusting speculation based on people's health records? Are they gathering data on us? She types in those famous names again, paying closer attention to the causes of death, knowing this can't be true. But, like so much online, it's a blend of squalid and boring and addictive, as if a stranger's apartment door were ajar, and she'd walked in, opened cupboards, read private letters. What she's doing feels like a violation – but only if she believes it. Or perhaps only if she's caught. Thankfully, nobody knows, she thinks. *Unless my searches are being recorded somehow.* Everyone has this paranoia since Leakzilla. The safest approach, all the tech experts say, is to behave as if someone's watching you at all times. And so she readies her defense: 'I knew the site was fake and vile. I was just trying to figure it out.' She checks the deaths of Lady Gaga and Andy Rosner and Mark Zuckerberg. Feels dirty to do so. But she can't stop, now typing in the names of law professors and fellow students.

What nonsense this is! Yet, if she's really so skeptical, why not enter the names of her family and friends? Or type in Bryan's name?

She won't. Yet Kelly does try her own – and the answer is a relief, a result so outlandish as to break the spell. She snorts at having been sucked in. Never once would she contemplate harming herself. If God allowed, she'd keep on living for ten thousand years. Moreover, self-harm violates her Christian faith; the body is a sacred gift.

As if awakening, she's suddenly staring at a crappy Nineties website, programmed by some freak with *way* too much free time. 'They seriously shouldn't allow stuff like this,' she mutters to her screen, and seeks the contact info for this page. Nothing gives away who's behind it. She types in her name again. Same result: 'Self-inflicted death'. Calmed, she closes the page, and gets down to work.

After hours of case law, Kelly takes a breather, stepping out to atone for her ghoulish surfing with an act of kindness.

Bryan is working a late shift, so she'll bring him dinner. She stocks up on overpriced Whole Foods pseudo-goodness, rolling her eyes at the product descriptions and the prices, then drives over to Tenleytown, where he works as a nursing-home orderly.

He handed in his resignation last month, but agreed to stay until they replaced him. He's responsible that way – and much loved by the residents. Bryan is far more tender than she, the rare guy who is truly shaken by violence. He couldn't get ten minutes into the Netflix documentary on the Newtown massacre. 'If they'd had an armed guard,' Kelly said at the time, 'it wouldn't have happened. You can't deny that, Bry.' In peculiar contrast to his sensitivity, Bryan draws gruesome phantasmagoric art that he sells as custom logos for Harleys and as cover art for indie video games. What began as a hobby in high school has unexpectedly become his main earner. With Bryan going full-time with his freelance art, they'll need a larger home with an office for him – and, he adds, space for when they start a family.

In the nursing-home day room, Kelly greets a few familiar residents. Old ladies in wheelchairs around a bridge table call her over, recognizing 'the brownie girl', as they've named her – not, as a nurse once awkwardly worried, because of her skin color but because of the plastic container of one-bite brownies that Kelly always brings in. She opens the lid, allowing arthritic fingers to reach in, pince one, lift sweetness to dry old lips. 'Take another. Help yourself. They're free.'

She was raised to respect her elders, and still recalls her grandfather's war stories. The fact that Kelly listened to his recollected capers, Boo has always said, is the reason Grandpa loved her so much, despite never before having trusted 'colored folk', as he called them. When Kelly distributes the brownies, she smiles at everyone, but grows sadder: these people should be cared for by their families. Then again, she and Bryan couldn't look after a senior at home. Who has space? Or time?

She inquires about an absent regular, Mr. Brickmann, the

curmudgeonly ninety-something Jewish man of Viennese birth who always looked her over with rheumy eyes, joking that he'd romance her away from Bryan yet!

'Oh, poor Mr. Brickmann. He isn't doing so good,' a Filipino nurse informs Kelly. 'He can't last so long, my darling. I'm sorry.' Apparently, it's chronic obstructive pulmonary disease, and he's in the final stages. There's no way back.

Bryan is waving for her to join him outside in the peace garden. They sit there, he gobbling the turkey burger and bean salad, she distracted by her online searches, of which she says nothing. Who tells of all that they've seen on the internet once back in the real world? And what she saw was clearly false. Yet, if it *was* false, why not enter Bryan's name? She watches him chew, metal-rimmed glasses rising up and down, his endearing wink when he sees she's observing him. She'll watch that face every day until the pulverizing instant when one of them is left in a home like this. Kelly winces to imagine anything ever happening to her man – it's too painful even to conceive.

'I should get back,' he says, his goodbye kiss tasting of turkey burger.

Upon returning to their apartment, Kelly immediately flips open her MacBook, tucks her hair behind one ear, then does the other – and types a fresh name into that site. The cursor blinks irritably; she isn't hitting enter yet. Not from fear but in rebellion, annoyed to waste time on this. The search box contains the full name of Mr. Brickmann. If the answer is 'chronic obstructive pulmonary disease', something disturbing is going on here.

Instead, the site burps out a random response: 'Traffic accident'. She stands up fast, exhaling with relief. No way Mr. Brickmann is driving again. The man can't get out of bed. The site is nonsense. She erases her browser history, and expunges the stupid experience from her mind. Well, almost. Falling asleep beside Bryan that night, she keeps seeing Héctor on the hospital bed, his stomach draining into that bag. How could the website know to answer 'Cirrhosis'?

Bryan has his final shift at the nursing home and – in

typical Bryan fashion – stays late to do unpaid overtime. A crazy day, he explains, once back at the apartment. 'Werner was not enjoying life, so it's a mercy in a way.' Mr. Brickmann's daughter collected him that day for the move to her home in New York State, where he was to pass away in peace. 'Thankfully, she was fine. Her car was totaled, though.'

Kelly's pulse quickens. When Bryan falls asleep reading his phone, Kelly – mind scrambling – sneaks away to her laptop, setting up on the breakfast bar, ferociously typing in names of school friends and school enemies, ex-room-mates, high-school volleyball coaches. A jolt of guilt hits her each time she reads a cause of death. Every few minutes, she enters her own name. Finally, she tries Bryan's.

Upon reading the answer, she hurries back into the bedroom, looking at him asleep, *refusing* to believe this. These are *not* facts! They aren't even alternative facts. Or even probabilities. But for Bryan, it said the same as her: 'Self-inflicted death'.

There's no way. No way. And yet it seems more plausible somehow, if they both were to do it. But *why?* We never would. Never. I know me; I know him. She shakes her head, repudiating this. *No.* What's the source of this information? The internet? I am *not* buying this.

But she can't tell him. She won't ever. Kelly has always been the skeptical partner; he, the innocent. She's not surrendering her role in this relationship. Nor is she pointlessly scaring the hell out of him. Because it's nonsense. Obviously. Right? Her fingers press the backlit Mac keyboard, the letter 'k' repeating across the screen, line after line.

She cannot study. The next day isn't any better. Her work requires being online – for the digital-law clinic, she still needs to pore over millions of these Leakzilla emails. But she can't be on the internet without returning compulsively to that website. Each time she passes faculty members at G. W. Law – those whose names she has already looked up, whose deaths she knows – Kelly scurries away, avoiding even a polite word. With classmates, it's the same. She's like that doctor who visited Héctor in bed, seeing death before the patient himself could. That is Kelly's existence now: walking into rooms, people smiling at her, unaware.

Bryan's older brother visits from Florida, to show his two sons around the capital. The youngest is having a tough time back in Tampa, tormented by a school bully called Jimmy-Ron DuPre. Shortly after they arrive, Kelly breaks away, saying she must fire off a law-clinic email, and takes her laptop into the bathroom, where she types in the bully's name. The result: 'Asphyxiation'. Disgusting herself, she cannot resist trying the names of those two little boys in the next room. The same result: 'Asphyxiation'. She is nauseated, confused.

She snaps shut the MacBook lid, unable to take this in. What is happening? Chewing her fingernails, she stares down at the bathroom tiles, chest thudding, needing to call Boo. She types in her sister's proper name, reading: 'Gunshot wound'. Kelly looks away, shaking her head. She clenches and unclenches her fists. I'm losing my goddamn mind. This isn't true.

'What, babe?' Bryan calls from the other room.

'No, nothing. Nothing.'

Someone must've hacked this computer, she decides, hearing the two little boys squeaking with laughter in the other room. Asphyxiation.

Kelly logs on to Facebook, and scans the profiles of her friends. When kids are mentioned, she types their names into the website. Each time, it's the same: 'Asphyxiation'. Frantically, she trawls news stories, harvesting names of strangers' children, such as a trio of Afghan girls in a *Washington Post* article about a school of orphans who escaped the Taliban. In each case, the answer is the same: 'Asphyxiation'.

Bryan knocks. She opens and sidesteps past him, claiming an upset stomach. 'I still have work. Sorry. I'll go into the bedroom.'

Why asphyxiation? Why only children? It's as if something is going to happen, far enough away that none of today's adults will be here for it. Just young people, then grown. But what? What happens next? This is crazy! Stop thinking this way!

Once Bryan's relatives have gone, he flops on the bed beside Kelly, kisses her neck, gives a goofy smirk. But she won't have sex in this frame of mind.

In the weeks that follow, Kelly remains cold, trapped in her thoughts, and turning down his advances. He gives up trying – something's bothering her, but Bryan has never been talented at figuring out what. He makes guesses, all wildly off the mark. However, he couldn't possibly know, this time. He starts to worry that they're breaking up. Maybe we're *not* together forever. 'Do you not like having me around the apartment this much? Because it feels that way. Ever since I left my job. Is that why, Kell? Did you want me to stay working there?'

'You're welcome in your own apartment, Bryan. Obviously.'

Both sit at their computers, opposite sides of the living room. She glances at law-school emails, unsure if this degree even makes sense anymore. Is planning for the future rational? She always knew, of course, that everyone dies. Why does knowing *how* make a difference? When younger, Kelly always figured herself perfect for military intelligence – the job is knowing what's around the corner, and she's forward-looking, prepared by nature. But now she knows something, and is crippled.

Even Bryan's upcoming departure for a comic convention causes her to fret, as if something could happen when they're apart, that everything's off-kilter, out of control. He hates flying, so will be driving all the way to Chicago. She's welcome to come along – always is, anywhere he goes. And his road trip coincides with her term break, so it provides a chance to escape this claustrophobic apartment, this claustrophobic city, to freshen themselves with the real America outside the Beltway.

During the long drive, Bryan keeps taking jokey detours to any piece of kooky Americana along the way. He claims it inspires his drawings, and he does sketch during stops. But it's also a matter of his humor – he can't drive past a sign promising 'World's Biggest Otter Statue!' without slamming on the brakes. 'We *got* to, Kells.'

Every quirky-sounding town, he diverts to, grinning all the way there. They stop at Altoona; Cuyahoga Falls; Shipshewana. Today, the detour is Paw Paw. Staring out the car window, Kelly almost returns to sanity, watching passing trees, tarmac rushing by. She turns to Bryan, considering his face — and experiences a surge of longing to make love to him, as if they're already old, and she's looking back at this moment, remembering trips like this in long-past days.

He takes a turn-off to grab coffee, following signs up I-94 toward Kalamazoo, parking at a strip mall with a Starbucks. They join the queue of college students, irascible senior citizens, crotchety soccer moms. Everyone's on edge this afternoon because a customer keeps insisting that his vanilla frap tastes like a caramel frap. With heroic patience, the heavyset barista offers to remake the drink yet again, checking verbally that every ingredient is exactly as desired.

On receiving the beverage, the customer sips, grimaces. 'Tastes funny.'

Everyone in line groans, and Kelly's mobile rings. It's that Hawaiian guy from the hospital who sneaked her Héctor's details. He took her contact information, too, and makes chit-chat now – he's trying to ask her out, she thinks. But it turns out to be a question about billing that he should probably pose to Héctor. 'Oh, I'm sorry,' the Hawaiian responds. 'That patient sadly passed.' He's calling to ask if she knows who's responsible for the bills, which amount to $743,302.14.

'Good of you guys to remember those fourteen cents.'

'Just how the computer shows it. I'm happy to send you the forms, if you know suitable family members. We can arrange installments.'

'Sorry – I need to go.'

The heavyset barista is beaming at her. 'What can I do you for today?'

She glimpses his peppy name-tag – 'Glen!' – imagines

typing it in, reading his fate. She mumbles, 'What am I doing here?'

'Might I suggest one of our seasonal specialties?'

At a motel outside Chicago, Kelly and Bryan lie side by side on a squeaky bed. They haven't had sex in weeks, and are fully dressed. She wants to say something; he wants to kiss something. For the umpteenth time, he asks what's bugging her. Law school? Where we'll live? To interrupt his questions, she kisses back – then pauses to ensure they have protection. 'We never agreed to get pregnant, Bry.'

'I accept that. Just got my hopes up. But, alrighty, I'll get my hopes down again.'

'Is it even fair to bring a child into the world right now?'

'Hey, the world would be way better with our kid in it.'

'Stuff just feels like it's going berserk.'

'Where?'

'Everywhere. You don't feel that?'

'Maybe our kid will be the one to fix it.' He looks directly at her, turning serious: 'Kelly, are we done, you and me?'

'What are you *talking* about?' she responds, excessively angry. 'What does that even mean?'

'You don't want kids with me. That means something. A lot, actually.'

She sits upright, nearly in tears, needing to explain what she cannot say.

Suddenly, they're united by both happening to stare at a terrible painting on the opposite wall: a trawler boat dragging a net. Bryan loves bad art. He smirks at her. 'Fisher?'

'What's that? Another name?'

'Yeah, and it'd work for a boy *or* a girl.' He waves it off. 'Sorry. This is just hurting myself now. Self-inflicted cruelty. We're not really a couple anymore. Are we?'

She excuses herself. Shut in the toilet, she draws the mobile from her back pocket, logs on to the website, types in 'Fisher Haas Michelmore'. The Wi-Fi connection is slow. Finally, an answer: no such name. There you go. They'll never have that child. Should she feel relieved? She doesn't. Kelly returns, lies perfectly still beside Bryan.

'What about "Lee"?' he says.

She lets him kiss her – then claims a need to quickly brush her teeth. Her electric toothbrush whirrs on its own in the sink as she types in a new name: 'Lee Haas Michelmore'. And there's a hit this time.

She turns off her phone fast, trying not to have seen the word that came after. She flicks off the toilet light. Just the whirring brush now. She comes out, looks at Bryan. We have a child. Waiting for us.

That site, she decides, with all its revolting claims – it's not real. It's a prank. Or a mindless algorithm. And *we* are not algorithms. *We* have free will. We *choose* what happens next. Right? 'Asphyxiation'. The cause of death beside that name glares in her mind. She shakes it from memory, reaching for Bryan's arm, his hand, his thighs. She sits astride him, both of them still fully dressed, but hurriedly changing that.

After sex, he flattens his palm on her naked belly, saying, 'Lee.'

Facts are not true sometimes, Kelly reminds herself.

She closes her hand over Bryan's, pressing his fingers against her softness, holding, hanging on. We will not stop ourselves.

We can't.

ALSO AVAILABLE

The Imperfectionists

TOM RACHMAN

'*The Imperfectionists* is alternately hilarious and heart-wrenching, and it's assembled like a Rubik's cube . . . a cross between Evelyn Waugh's *Scoop* and Hunter S. Thompson's *Fear and Loathing* adventure . . . so good I had to read it twice'

New York Times Book Review

'So beautifully written, so compassionate in its observation and understanding of human behaviour, that one cannot tear the eyes from the page'

The Times

ALSO AVAILABLE

The Rise and Fall of Great Powers

Tom Rachman

'Some novels are such good company that you don't want
them to end; Tom Rachman knows this, and has pulled off
the feat of writing one'
Sunday Telegraph

'Mesmerising: a thorough work-out for the head and heart
that targets cognitive muscles you never knew you had'
The Times